TEMPTATION

Stuart held Danita's hand, then gently pressed her against his body, her head resting on his chest. He didn't want to scare her, but she had to know that he found her attractive. She had to know that he wanted her. No Lowell had ever married a Godfrey, but had there ever been an attraction like this?

She looked up and saw the fire in his dark, sensual eyes. She'd seen him angry, calm, and everything in between, but never had she been exposed to the raw sexuality of the man. Still, she challenged him by not trying to escape his grasp. She nodded her agreement. But Danita knew, if anything happened between them, it would be Danita's decision.

TEMPTATION

Viveca Carlysle

BET Publications, LLC
www.bet.com
www.arabesquebooks.com

ARABESQUE BOOKS are published by

BET Publications, LLC
c/o BET BOOKS
One BET Plaza
1900 W Place NE
Washington, D.C. 20018-1211

All Kensington Titles, Imprints, and Distributed Lines are available at special quantity discounts for bulk purchases for sales promotions, premiums, fund-raising, and educational or institutional use. Special book excerpts or customized printings can also be created to fit specific needs. For details, write or phone the office of the Kensington special sales manager: Kensington Publishing Corp., 850 Third Avenue, New York, NY 10022, attn: Special Sales Department, Phone: 1-800-221-2647.

First Printing: March 2001
10 9 8 7 6 5 4 3 2 1

Printed in the United States of America

One

The torrential rains pounded the beach and demolished the oceanfront homes for three days and nights. The heart-wrenching destruction showed on the faces of families as they watched all they possessed float out to sea and disappear beneath the seemingly mile-high waves. Their earthly goods vanished in only an instant. In spite of man's attempt to outwit her, Mother Nature ruled.

Stuart Lowell struggled to keep his emotions in check as he stood on the mezzanine and watched his staff grab the evening clothes from the racks and pile them into plastic bags. The broken window meant everything on the first floor was ruined. He glanced at his watch. The seven A.M. display seemed unreal. Usually when items stopped selling they were shipped to one of the resale stores or charity auctions. That would not be the case now. Lowell's Malibu was about to have its first ever markdown sale.

For Stuart, this could not have happened at a more critical time in his career. The annual summit meeting, as the Godfreys and Lowells called it, a week at his father's Virginia estate, where the executives talked about their stores and the children participated in games that would later sharpen their wits in the world of business, was only three months away. His store would not have time to recover. It would take that long to assess the damage and develop a new plan of action.

He rolled up his sleeves and headed for the stairs to join his crew, when his secretary leaned out of the office and called to him.

"Tyler Godfrey's on the phone. He says it's urgent."

Stuart quickly retraced his steps and returned to his office. "Thanks. He probably wants to know the damage."

Stuart went to his office and picked up the phone. "Hello, Tyler. How's New York?"

"Find out for yourself. I want you here tomorrow. Got a surprise."

"Tyler, we just had a storm wreck the store. . . ."

"I know. I watch the news. Let Dax earn his keep for a change. See you tomorrow."

Before he could respond, the phone went dead. Tyler had been known to hang up like that when he didn't want anyone to argue with him. But he used that technique only when he had something really important to discuss, and so twenty minutes later, Stuart had dictated his assignments to his secretary and headed home to break the news to Dax.

Tyler Godfrey had announced his plans to retire from running the New York store and Stuart was sure he would name his successor at the upcoming summit meeting. As much as he loved his California life, Stuart wanted the jewel in the Lowell's chain—Lowell's NY.

Until the storm, he knew that his store had the best sales record in the chain. Now the family might see him as the only one who could recoup the losses and feel he should stay in California. If that happened, Lowell's NY would go to his greatest competitor—Danita Godfrey.

Even though it was a Sunday, Danita Godfrey was still thinking about all the work she could be doing in D.C. Her fingers drummed an impatient tune on the armrest of the huge green and white plaid chair by the fireplace in the living room of her uncle Tyler's Harlem Brownstone. It was similar to the studio apartment attached to his office at the store. There had been family stories about how he would work until he was too tired to go home and then have Jolene, his live-in housekeeper, come in to cook meals in the tiny kitchen.

Danita was waiting for her uncle Tyler to join her. He'd called the night before and asked her to come see him, and no matter how she cajoled, he wouldn't tell her why. It sounded as if

he had something important to tell her. It left
room for good and bad scenarios to run
through her mind.

Perhaps he hadn't decided that she was the
one to take over Lowell's NY. She brushed that
thought from her mind as quickly as it had appeared. Of course she was his choice. She'd
been the one tagging after him, learning how
he ran the business, since she was a skinny sixth-
grader. By the time she was in high school, she
was sitting in on board meetings with him. She
had to be the one.

At twenty-six, she'd been handed the reins to
Lowell's D.C., and in three years she had created the premiere store for D.C.'s elite. On the
fifth floor of her store she placed the brightly
colored, cutting-edge fashions of the new designers; on the sixth floor, the reserved and classical
designs of Oscar de la Renta and Bill Blass.

The fifth floor was now a gathering place for
the young, daring D.C. workforce. The designers
had more space to show their wares. Even the
piped in music had the same driving beat and
cutting-edge style as the designers. Prior to her
arrival this section had been relegated to a
small, hidden area of the store.

The sixth floor catered to a more mature
crowd. Things moved slower. Customers were
given time to browse. Even the sales staff were
older and more comfortable with the clothes
and accessories on this floor.

Three months after Danita took over she began having special events. She tried to have them every three months but after the second one, she decided that events shouldn't be that close together.

The other feather in her cap had come when she was dating a congressman. After watching some of the newly elected officials and their wives commit faux pas at the steady stream of parties and dinners they attended, Danita hired Elianna Wilson, an Englishwoman of African descent, to give etiquette classes. They were like those given by the wealthy. Word of mouth spread quickly, and the classes were booked solid for the upcoming year. They weren't advertised, but the private classes for adults were a popular staple of Lowell's D.C. too.

She loved the store, and there was no reason she shouldn't be Tyler's successor and pilot the New York store. But no matter how she tried to bolster her spirit, there was a little voice in the back of her mind chanting that Tyler really called her here to tell her privately that Lowell's NY would *not* be hers.

Tyler Godfrey's voice brought her back to the present. "Sorry, I've been on the phone with that new chauffeur. He's lost again. Don't know why I hired him."

Danita grinned and then said, "Yes you do. He's the grandson of your college buddy."

"Right. The only time I do a favor, and this is what I get. The boy has no sense of direction.

All he has to do is pick someone up at the airport and bring him here."

"Pick someone up?"

"Yeah. Stuart."

Tiny spikes of cold danced up and down Danita's spine. Why would he invite Stuart? Before she could ask, the chimes sounded.

"At last. He found the house."

Stuart joined them moments later. Although Danita insisted she wasn't affected by the man, she could understand why women threw themselves at him. His smooth ebony face had a healthy glow in spite of tiny lines around his eyes from squinting at the California sun. He was wise enough to use plenty of sunblock to prevent burning, she thought. So many African Americans thought their darkness deflected the harsh rays and allowed themselves to eschew any products they considered directed to fair-skinned people. Unfortunately, the result made them look older than their chronological age.

His hair was different from the last time she'd seen him. It was cut close to his head and quite curly. His frame had just enough muscle to make the navy pinstriped Armani suit look both tailored and comfortable.

Danita's eyes finally met his, and she saw the smile creep over his face. Her face grew hot as she realized he knew she'd perused his body, as most women did when they wanted to get his attention.

Without thinking, she opened the two buttons

on her black Donna Karan jacket and revealed
a red silk camisole-style blouse. It was a look
she'd felt most comfortable with and one that
took her from a day in the office to a night on
the town. But she seldom opened the jacket
during the day. Why was she doing so now, she
asked herself. Her face grew warmer when Stuart's eyes widened, and she quickly turned away.

If he was amused by the once-over she'd given
him, all amusement disappeared the moment
she opened her jacket. He'd always thought of
her as skinny, since she barely cleared five feet
and probably never weighed more than one
hundred pounds. He didn't realize how curva-
ceous a slender body could be until that moment. He certainly wasn't expecting the full
breasts enhanced by the brightly colored top.

Perhaps others had the same feelings Danita
experienced when she saw Stuart. His quiet, soft-
spoken style could be intimidating for those who
angered him and seductive when he intended it
to be so. Once, she'd considered him "family."
She treated him as she would an older brother
when they were growing up. An older, annoying
brother, since he liked to show how smart he
was by discussing world events, the economy,
and sports events with such authority that the
others in their age group hung on his every
word. But her relationship with Stuart changed
when her father let one of his numerous liaisons
become public. It was amazing what her mother

and the rest of the Godfreys and Lowells would accept as long as it wasn't public knowledge.

She was twelve and it was during a summit meeting. She'd followed her mother's advice to hold her head high and not to mention her father at all. When she took a stroll by the lake, she'd run into Stuart.

"I . . . uh . . . heard about your father."

"I don't want to talk about it."

"I know, it's hard when your father has a lot of girlfriends. I guess if my father acted like a jerk—"

Danita had attacked, swinging her small fists and trying to pummel him into the ground. "Don't you ever call my father a jerk," she screamed. It wasn't so much that he called her father a jerk. She lashed out because he knew. He knew that there was more than one. Maybe if her father had only one girlfriend, she could have forgiven him. She felt as if all the times he said he loved her were a lie. He couldn't love her and do this.

Stuart had only grabbed her arms and held her as she cried. She pulled away, ran back to the house, and hid in her room for most of the day. She'd never forgiven him for making her feel so helpless.

They avoided each other as much as possible after that, and even when they had to be together for business reasons, they kept their distance. They had learned to be polite and chat just enough so that no one knew what had passed between them.

She'd become an overachiever, trying to prove she could play with the big boys and win. Her reputation was that of a tough negotiator, but she managed not to become hard.

Her father had wanted the New York store, but because of his indiscretions, Tyler had been called from Virginia to take over. That's why she felt the New York store was *her* legacy. She would erase her father's cheating from her mind. She would never talk about it, and maybe everyone else would stop, and one day she would get Lowell's NY.

Now, as they stood in Tyler's living room, she felt claustrophobic. Stuart walked over to her, took her hand, and brought it to his lips. He always greeted her that way. At first she thought he was mocking her because her father had exiled himself to Paris, and he was being continental, but later she realized he wasn't the type to kiss women on the cheek, and the hand was easier.

Some of her female friends had insisted there was something romantic in his actions, and after his divorce they encouraged Danita to go after him.

As one friend put it: "You two are so right for each other, you don't even see it."

When she protested, the woman just uttered that old saw about "not seeing the forest for the trees or feeling the wind for the breeze."

Danita had never let her mind wander in that direction. It was ironic that in all the years of the partnership, no Godfrey had ever married a Lowell. There had been several matchmaking attempts, but somehow it just never happened. Stuart wasn't her type no matter what any of the others said.

Now she found herself four years from thirty with no man on the horizon. She told herself that would change once Tyler announced his successor. Then she would have time for romance. She'd had long-term relationships with men who were as ambitious as she. When their careers took them out of the D.C. area, she had chosen not to follow. She wasn't hearing a biological clock ticking, as some of her friends did, so she was comfortable with her social life. Even if her mother had more than hinted she worked too much, Danita had insisted, "I'll know when to give it up."

Jolene arrived and ushered Tyler, Stuart and Danita into the dining room, where they sat down to enjoy steaming grits, scrambled eggs, crisp bacon, and buttermilk biscuits. Tyler's housekeeper had studied the culinary arts all over the world, but her best still came from her southern roots. They didn't talk much as they savored the meal. Danita wondered if she got the New York store, could she steal Jolene away also?

Tyler knew that this was the only time Danita and Stuart allowed themselves the luxury of breakfast. Their workaholic lifestyles didn't leave room for more than toast, juice, and coffee before rushing off to work. He'd watched them closely and wondered if his plan for them would succeed. It wasn't the first time he'd played cupid, but with these two, there was a slight chance he'd miscalculated.

Danita tried to pretend she enjoyed the food so much there was no room for conversation, but inwardly, she seethed about Stuart being anywhere in her vicinity. Her childhood memories of Stuart were those of constant competition during summit weeks. Stuart always seemed to set the pace. He was the one who found a new twist on old games. He was the one who excelled in everything effortlessly. Danita had tried to avoid him, but rich history linked their families forever.

New York was a mecca for African Americans in the 1920's and 1930's, from the poetry of Langston Hughes to the plays of Zora Neale Hurston to the stage presence of Paul Robeson, a time when African Americans ventured out and took pride in their accomplishments. Harlem was the place to be and be seen.

It was the time of Duke Ellington's music, and the Cotton Club was the hottest nightclub around. That's where Jacob Godfrey and Frank Lowell met. The men became fast friends and then partners in a small store. They had big dreams, and on a toss of a coin named the store Lowell's. The store expanded as the clientele grew. It catered to the needs of artists and musicians, and even the daughter of America's first black self-made millionaire, Madam C. J. Walker, was a frequent visitor to Lowell's.

Jacob Godfrey and Frank Lowell had teamed up to open the small general store and barbershop, called Jake and Frank's. Over the years the barbershop had closed and the store became a department store. The store remained in Harlem until 1970 and the second generation took over the day-to-day operations. In the 1980's the expansion began and didn't stop until each of the ten descendants was in charge of a store. The name changed slightly by adding the location initials, Lowell's NY, Lowell's D.C., Lowell's CA, etc., and now there was the recently added beachside boutique, Lowell's Malibu.

Danita's mind traveled over the history and expansion of Lowell's and back to the present problem of who would be Tyler's successor. The gatherings referred to as summit meetings were in fact a series of competitions as to whose store had the best merchandise, who had contributed most to the Lowell's image, or whose children were the smartest or best behaved.

The rivalry was almost as fierce as that of the Hatfields and McCoys. No one could remember how it started, but throughout the years it had brought out the best and worst of the families.

Danita had taken only small portions of the food on the table. She pretended her size was the reason she couldn't each much. In fact, she had to watch what she ate because she didn't want anyone to know that the stress of running the store had given her the beginnings of an ulcer. The doctor had warned her it would get progressively worse, but that hadn't stopped her from wanting to replace Tyler as CEO and control all the Lowell's stores. *Once I get New York, I can slow down,* she told herself. It was the stress of not knowing where she stood that made her have a nervous stomach, she now convinced herself.

She glanced at Stuart and Tyler. They weren't having any of the problems she experienced. Stuart's appetite made her wonder if he had one of those naturally overactive metabolisms or if this meant hours of exercise when he returned to California.

She waited as the two men settled back with strong black coffee to finish the meal. Jolene had provided Danita with herbal tea. The woman was almost psychic when it came to feeding the Godfreys and the Lowells.

After almost ten years at Lowell's CA, Stuart was definitely the pacesetter for the rest of the vice presidents. Beverly Hills was the perfect spot for him. He met and married an up-and-coming starlet. Two years ago, after their divorce, Stuart came up with the idea of a boutique for the beach crowd, and Lowell's Malibu was born. If it hadn't been for the storm, he'd be the star at the summit meeting once again.

Now they sat in Tyler's brownstone, slightly disheartened. Deep in her heart she felt that Stuart represented the son Tyler had lost. But she was a Godfrey, and why shouldn't another Godfrey replace Tyler?

Tyler's only son had been killed during the Korean War. She was now his closest relative.

When Tyler first started talking about retiring, the rumors flew hot and heavy and the candidates were Danita's aunt, who ran the Dallas office, and Stuart's uncle, who had so much success with the Boston store. Their had even been talk of going outside the families and selecting Morgan Sylvester. He'd married Danita's cousin, and together they handled the day-to-day activity at Lowell's GA in Atlanta.

Sometimes Danita wondered where Stuart got his ambition. Certainly not from his father, who enjoyed the laid-back lifestyle of Lowell's VA. He hated to leave the state so much, he'd opened his home to the summit meeting rather than having to travel.

Each of the stores had some type of success story, but not all the vice presidents aspired to the hustle and bustle of New York. In fact, there were more who wanted to stay at their current locations than there were candidates for Tyler's spot.

Danita knew why she and Stuart were in competition. He probably felt the same way she did when she interned with Tyler. She'd fallen in love with the city. Washington, D.C., was also an exciting city, but she felt she'd done all she could with the store there. New York was the largest and the flagship store. She just had to have it.

Although they were only six years apart in age, Danita felt she was living in Stuart's shadow. When she earned her MBA from Harvard, Stuart had already done that. When she created the etiquette classes, he'd created the Malibu boutique. He was also a much-sought-after bachelor and hadn't embarrassed the family by behaving badly in public. Danita felt she was still trying to live down her father's outrageous acts. Darius and Elizabeth Godfrey's marriage was over.

That was another reason she wanted to move to New York. Even now, fourteen years after the fact, some newspapers identified her as the daughter of the man who had had an affair with a congressman's wife. It became public knowledge when Danita's father left her mother, moved to Paris, and had his lover follow him there.

The affair that was so hot in the nation's capital seemed to have cooled abroad, and the woman returned to the States in disgrace. Danita's father wisely stayed in France, and she spoke to him not more than once a year since what she called "the incident."

D.C. could be an unforgiving city, and despite

all the years that had passed, people never let her forget her father's indiscretions. The scandal stigma never let go of anyone, but New Yorkers didn't seem to be as concerned about it as the rest of the world.

Ever since his sixty-fifth birthday, Tyler had threatened to retire, but somehow his rumblings this year had been taken seriously. If he'd had a child to succeed him, he might have retired early, as most of the other board members did, and passed the mantle to his child. But Tyler's only son had been killed during the Korean conflict, and most felt the old man needed the store to keep him going.

Despite all the success in the individual stores, most of the contenders wanted the prestige of running the flagship store. Now that Tyler was retiring, it appeared someone's dream was about to come true.

"How did Dax take it?" Tyler asked gruffly.

"Not too well. I hope we still have a store when I get back."

"You let Dax run the store?" Danita's eyes widened as she stared at Stuart and waited for an answer.

"Stop acting as if he's a total incompetent. He was a little nervous until I said the magic words."

"And those magic words are?" Danita asked.

"It's only for a few days."

Danita and Stuart laughed because of all the people in their combined families, Dax always said he'd never be one of those button-down executives.

"Not so," Tyler said.

"What does that mean?" Danita asked.

"It means that I need the two of you in New York and Dax will have to run the store for the next ninety days."

"Ninety days?" Stuart's fear flashed across his face.

"Don't you think Stuart needs to be there to guide Dax—"

"No. The boy needs to learn how to make some tough decisions."

"Now?"

"Yes. Now."

Danita remembered how she, Stuart, and their counterparts started out. As soon as they graduated from college, each had worked in New York. Tyler was an instinctively good businessman, and interning with him wasn't easy or financially rewarding. But she had learned the business and developed a love for it. Dax had never loved anything about the store. The problem was, he hadn't shown signs of loving anything that could sustain him long enough to make a living.

For a moment Danita thought it would be a good idea for Stuart to return to California. It would give her a chance to be with Tyler and convince him that she was worthy of the New York store. But she couldn't do it. That wouldn't have been fair.

"What exactly are we going to be doing for three months?"

"Getting my Sag Harbor house ready for sale."

"You're kidding, Tyler. There's no way I'm going to leave Dax alone for three months. That's right about summit meeting time."

"I'm with Stuart. Uncle Tyler, we can't possibly take that much time away from our stores. Why don't you hire one of those services?"

"Because they won't know what's worth keeping."

"This sounds like something you should be there handling. You can assemble the things you want to keep and let them get rid of the rest of the stuff."

"Can't. Tried it and got lost in memories. You two would be better at it. You know the family history. I trust you. I'm asking for a favor."

That was the most important thing Tyler Godfrey had said. Trust was important to all of them. It was a special time when they were pushed out of the nest and given a store to manage. It meant Tyler trusted them. Now he was saying he trusted them with something even more precious.

"I don't mind, but . . ." Stuart took a deep breath before continuing. "Danita and I don't exactly work well together."

"Then it's time you learned how. Tell you what; I know that everyone is interested in who's taking my place when I retire. Well, the truth is the other members on the board know it's going to be one of you. But it takes more than talent and guts. Believe me, I know you both have that. I'm not saying this is a contest, but what if you were in my place? Do you know how many in this family I can't stand the sight of?"

Tyler had never indicated whom he disliked. He loved Danita and Stuart, but he wasn't disgruntled about anyone else, including Dax, who seemed to thrive on getting on people's nerves.

"I don't want just anyone handling Mary's things."

They knew he wasn't just tugging at their heartstrings. Tyler had always been fussy about the Sag Harbor house even after his wife died and he moved to the Harlem brownstone, not far from where it all started. That store was now a high-rise, but it was part of Lowell's history.

"We don't mind helping out, but we're both compiling figures for the annual meeting, and that's really not the time to be away. How about a compromise?"

"Okay. What's a good time frame? How about two months?"

"How about three weeks?"

"You haven't been up to the house lately," Tyler explained. "It's not going to be easy."

"We know. Give us a week to put things together for the staff," Danita said. "And I want one more thing."

"What's that?"

"Your successor gets New York, we know that, but I want you to promise that whoever you don't choose gets to pick his . . . or her . . . consolation prize."

Tyler and Stuart exchanged looks that said they didn't get it.

"It'll be a win, win, win situation for all of us."

Stuart nodded. He was getting a different view of this woman. The gossip at Lowell's D.C. had gotten back to all the Lowells and Godfreys. Danita Godfrey was one tough lady when she negotiated anything for her store. He was beginning to see a sliver of that.

"Can you give me a hint of what you mean?"

"Not really. I guess we won't know what the second choice is until we have to make it."

Tyler's wrinkled face broke into a huge grin. "I'm going to agree, but I hope I haven't been sucker-punched. Okay, you move into the house and pack it up."

Stuart folded his arms across his chest. "I still have a problem. I can't leave Dax alone for three weeks. He'll be calling me every hour asking what he should do."

"Stuart's right. Dax won't do a good job alone."

Stuart turned to her and smiled. The woman was full of surprises. She'd grown more confident since the last time he'd seen her. She'd missed a couple of the summit meetings and her mother stood in for her. He'd begun to believe she was afraid to show up. Then a "reliable source" in her office had told him that Danita was interested in the New York store.

Now, here she was, knowing that he was the enemy, and fighting for him to stay in the game. He admired a woman who wasn't afraid of the competition.

"You got a better idea?" Tyler was challenging Danita.

She thought about it for a moment and then smiled. "Why don't we send someone who can whip him into shape and lead him down the right path?"

"Sounds good. Then you and Stuart can be back here in a week. Who do you have in mind?"

"You."

Two

Tyler roared with laughter. "Don't try that with me." The old man was still quick to recognize a con artist.

"You want us to take time from our schedule, don't you? Then you need to take time from yours," Danita said.

"It'll take me at least three weeks to slap that boy around."

"Then we'll spend three weeks getting the house ready," Stuart offered.

"Uncle Tyler, are you sure you want to sell the house?" Danita asked.

"I've been thinking about it for a few years. I'm not going to make the trip out there too often. When I retire, I don't want to be isolated. You need a car to get around that area. I'm getting too old to drive a lot. I really want to sell the house."

Danita couldn't believe he'd ever give up the beautiful house in Sag Harbor. He and Mary had given some lavish parties in that place. It was old-fashioned in design. It had been built about 1840 and was in the Greek Revival style. The four huge bedrooms each had a view; the two at the back looked out on a beautiful garden and the Olympic-size outdoor pool and small pool house. The two bedrooms at the front faced one of the two huge oak trees in the yard. What set it off was the white picket fence that ran around the entire property. During a particularly bad time in their lives, Danita and her mother had lived there to avoid the press. She hadn't been there for a few years, but she couldn't see the house belonging to anyone but a Godfrey or a Lowell. The thought of owning it herself flitted through her mind, but her life consisted of riding roughshod over Lowell's D.C. and finding more ideas to attract shoppers. She worked closely with almost every division, but the one she liked best was the Special Events. They had been setting up events for two years. Each month something was happening at the store to get good press.

"Did you try any of the family members? I mean, someone might want it for a summer home."

"No, they won't. It's just a little too isolated for the younger ones, and the older ones are already settled. Let it go on the market. Get some new blood in there."

"Then Danita and I will make sure you get the best deal possible."

Danita wasn't sure of that. Stuart had made it sound as if they were a team. They would never be a team. She held her peace only because she didn't want to upset Tyler.

"So we're all agreed. We'll meet back here in a week. Oh, one more thing. Don't tell Dax I'm coming. He might run off and hide in Mexico until you come back."

Danita and Stuart declined the offer of a chauffeur and decided to walk around Manhattan for a while.

"Tyler seemed a little upset with the chauffeur. Did the chauffeur have a problem?"

"I haven't been here in a couple of years, and I had to tell him how to get to Tyler's."

"How long has he been here?"

"All his life. But I think he's a new driver, and that could be a problem. When you walk or take the subway, you don't look at street signs. Then you get a license and suddenly one-way streets become very important." Stuart remembered learning to navigate around California.

"You're right. I think I'm going to remind Tyler of that."

Sunday was a good day for a casual stroll, since most of the offices were closed and the area was a prime tourist spot. Danita kept some distance between them so she didn't feel so tiny when she was with Stuart. She could understand why models liked to date him—they were tall enough so they didn't feel overpowered by him.

"Let's go over to Rockefeller Center," Stuart suggested.

"Why?"

"I think we need to talk about this whole thing."

She nodded. They kept their leisurely pace, and when they got to their destination found a granite bench in a shaded area.

"Do you think there's something more to what Tyler's doing?" he asked.

"I don't know. I think it's odd that he wants to sell the house. He and Mary were there for about forty years. That's a lot of memories. But I want to say just one thing. I don't know if we can work together."

"Why not?"

"We think differently."

"That might be a good thing."

Danita shook her head. "I want this to be a business deal."

"I guess we could pretend that we haven't known each other forever."

"We don't have to pretend. We *don't* know each other. What's my favorite color?"

He couldn't believe it. She was right. They had practically grown up together and he didn't know her favorite color. He was sure she didn't know his. "I see what you mean. So what should we do?"

"Just think of this as a business venture."

He nodded. "He's your uncle. Do you have

any vibes? Do you think he's worried about his health?"

"Could be. I get a feeling that there's more to this, but I don't think he's sick or anything. I just think there's something he's not telling us."

"It's a great house. I remember wanting to go there during summer break rather than to my dad's place."

"That's because every August all the families descended at your father's place for bloodletting."

"I think that's as much of real corporate life as Dad can stand."

As they talked, Danita knew he was going to bring up the time he tried to talk to her about her father. She still couldn't discuss it, so she searched her mind for another subject. "What's with your brother?"

"He's almost thirty going on eighteen. I don't know what to do with him. He'll get a real job long enough to make enough money to hang out with his buddies. He's a temporary agency's dream."

"Ever think of the 'tough-love' approach?"

"It's crossed my mind, but I know why he lost his enthusiasm. I even know when."

"What happened?"

"My parents were on his case pretty hard. He never had an aggressive personality, and they couldn't understand it. You know our families."

"Go for the jugular every time."

"Right. But Dax wasn't like that. He wanted people to like him, not be afraid of him."

"So when did you realize that?"

"He fell in love. He brought a girl home and I knew he was serious about her. She seemed pretty serious about him until she found out he wasn't going to have a high-powered job in Lowell's. She was looking for an upwardly mobile member of the community. Dax was an artist. He worked at Lowell's VA as the art director. He'd actually designed some of our best windows. It paid enough for him to live on. But the young lady was looking for more. When she found out that only the family members with business degrees moved into the vice presidencies, she turned her attention to me."

"You didn't?"

"Of course not. I barely spoke to her when I realized what she was doing. When Dax realized it, he just closed up. He became this freeloader type."

"He's the one who always seems to have the most fun. We're banging our heads against the wall, trying to prove we've done a good job, and he's out with the kids in the pool. They love him."

"He loves them. I hope Tyler can see something in him that I've missed."

Now she knew Stuart's concern for Dax wasn't just the running of the store. He knew his brother was running from life, and soon it would be too late for him to catch up. She'd seen it happen to a couple of family members. They now held menial jobs at one of the stores or worked for a big firm where they'd gotten lost and now were living from paycheck to paycheck.

"You know, he's the one who should be cleaning out Tyler's house. It might give him a sense of Lowell's history."

"I'm not too sure that would work. He might feel it's already too late. Look at what Dad and Tyler had accomplished by the time they were our ages."

The granite bench soon became uncomfortable, and they rose to leave. Danita was on her way back to the airport and Stuart was going to stay over in a hotel. He found a cab, gave directions, and paid for the trip before she could protest. LaGuardia Airport had shuttle flights on the hour, and she was home by six P.M.

Back in D.C., Danita pulled out a legal pad and a pen and curled up on the soft couch in her Georgetown apartment. Although she liked the computer, a pen and pad were the best methods of brainstorming for her. She wondered how she was going to break it to the person who would take her place if she got New York. Chris Lowell. He was going to be elated. He'd probably feel the way an understudy would when the star got food poisoning. It was going to be his big break. She wasn't going to tell him that it would be short-lived. Three weeks in Sag Harbor, and she'd be back in the driver's seat.

She wondered how her mother would take it. She'd been Danita's sounding board and the person who went to the summit meetings, but she didn't want to oversee the day-to-day operation of the store, so that job was given to Danita.

Two hours later, she was ready to transfer the final draft of her plans to train her replacement to the computer. That took another hour. She showered and climbed into bed. She usually slept naked. She made a mental note to buy some sleepwear the next day. Just before she drifted off to sleep, she remembered how easy it was to talk to Stuart as long as they didn't talk about her father.

Stuart was enjoying a movie in his hotel room. An action thriller with lots of car chases, shooting, and very few love scenes. He rarely got to do this in California. Most of the women he dated were interested in seeing deep, sensitive films. After making sure that everything was working in Lowell's CA and the Malibu boutique, he didn't want to have to think about whether the plot made sense.

He'd picked up his five messages, and three were from Dax. He hadn't been gone a full day, and his brother was already in a panic. He called and reassured him that he would be home the next day but refrained from telling him anything more. He had a message from the store that everything was under control, but it was the last message that was most disturbing. It was from his ex-wife. Dax had probably given her the number. Dax still had a soft spot for her, even if Stuart didn't.

Although he knew it was a bad move, he called her back. She spent the next half hour whining about her small monthly alimony check—which would feed the average family of four for a year. Then she started accusing him of deceiving her.

"You knew I wanted to have a beach house when we were married. You bought it because I'd have no claim to it," she railed, referring to the house Stuart purchased the day after the divorce became final.

"We've had this discussion before. You have a house that's paid for in Brentwood, and you got the car you wanted."

"I remortgaged the house. I can't make the payment."

"You did what? Why?"

"I wanted to help my career. Most deals are made at film festivals. I had to look good."

"Did you get any jobs while you were buying clothes and going to film festivals?"

"I got a pilot for a new series, but the networks changed their minds at the last minute. It was too sexy for regular TV and not sexy enough for cable. I just need that one break."

"I hope you get it." He meant it. He knew how hard she worked, but acting was one of those careers where talent didn't always get noticed. For black women there were fewer roles. When they were married, she'd wanted Stuart to back her in a picture deal, but he wouldn't. That's when the marriage began to fade.

"So, are you going to send me the money?"

"The money for what?"

"The mortgage payment. Haven't you been listening? I remortgaged the house."

"No. I left you with a house that was free and clear. If you lose it, I can't help it."

"How can you say that, when you have access to all that money. I read about Lowell's in the papers. You're worth millions."

"That's the corporation's money, not mine. Won't the alimony check pay the mortgage?"

"And what am I supposed to live on? Could you just lend me the money?"

"How much?" The figure she quoted was reasonable. He didn't plan to ask her to pay the money back, but he did tell her it was the last time he'd bail her out. She raged at him about having money and not sharing it. He let her vent, then very quietly said, "This isn't a loan. It's a gift, and it's the very last time I'm going to be this generous. If your career isn't supporting you, maybe it's time for a change."

She told him where to wire the money, and he promised he would do it the next morning. She thanked him, and again he told her it was the last time. At 9:00 A.M. the money was on its way, even before his flight.

* * *

A week later, Danita arrived at the airport and purchased her ticket for the shuttle. She felt strange about buying a one-way ticket, but she wasn't sure how she would travel in three weeks. She carried her suitcase with wheels and a larger tote bag. She'd gotten through the week with antacid tablets, but this morning she'd awakened with none of the symptoms of an ulcer. She'd enjoyed a large breakfast that had given her no trouble. Maybe her body considered this a vacation. She only took the tablets when stressful situations arose.

"Taking a trip, Ms. Godfrey?"

She turned to face one of the stringers for a local paper. The man was looking for dirt, and once he did the laundered version for the paper, there was always the titillating one that ended up in one of the rags. Years ago, someone just like him had made her life a living hell by trying to interview her when the scandal broke involving her father. She'd escaped this kind of thing until she started seeing the congressman. They never got a chance to go beyond a brief relationship, when a few public outings turned into a frenzy and the old nonsense was dredged up again.

"I'm visiting family."

"So do you think you'll be old Tyler Godfrey's replacement? Your company could use another woman on the board. How about an exclusive?

You tell me what's happening and you decide on your reward."

They announced her flight. "I'm visiting family. Good-bye." She walked to the gate but felt his eyes on her all the way. She refused to look back.

Stuart's flight had been uneventful and he hoped his short stay would be also. He had only a short time to get his team together. He was proud of the team he'd put together and he knew they could handle any situation. Stuart was sorry he hadn't put one of them in charge instead of Dax. Sometimes family loyalty got in the way at Lowell's but he hoped this time his brother would show his strength and that would make it easier to move to New York. Unfortunately Dax didn't see the challenge.

Stuart was having more trouble with Dax, who constantly hounded him about who was coming to handle the store.

"Why are you and Danita the ones to handle this?"

"Tyler's old and eccentric—leave it alone."

After condensing a month's work into a week, he was ready to clean out Tyler's house. It meant he would be completely out of touch. The main phones in the house had been turned off, but Tyler's private line was working. Stuart refused to give Dax the number. He flew back to New York that morning. Danita arrived in New York two hours later.

That night, when Stuart and Danita were safely ensconced in Tyler's Harlem brownstone, they were treated to Jolene's cooking while they finalized their plans.

"I swear, Tyler, I'm going to find a way to steal this woman," Danita said.

"Can you cook?" Stuart asked.

"Sure. Don't get any ideas. We will share the cooking and cleaning. I'm not going to spend a lot of time in the kitchen. Get ready for some easy recipes."

"I had Jolene stock the kitchen and pantry. There are local stores if you need anything else," Tyler told them. "I figure that you will spend most of your time in the house so you can finish the job."

"You can say that again. Three weeks is it. I don't care what's left to finish."

"Come on, Danita, don't be like that. If it takes us another week, we'll give it a shot."

She laughed, then said, "You just want Tyler to continue Dax's boot camp. Are you going to call him at any time?"

"I would love to be a fly on the wall when Tyler shows up, but I told my brother there was no way to contact me."

Breakfast the next morning was a little strange. She knew that this meal would be dif-

ferent when she came out of the guest room
and saw Stuart leaning against the bar, sipping
orange juice. It was amazing what happened
when a man who was always corporate changed
clothes. She'd seen him in business suits that
looked as if they were made for him. She'd
watched him walk into a room in a tux and
noticed how he made everyone's head turn.
Even at the summit meetings he wore casual but
tailored clothes. She had never seen him like
this. The well-worn jeans hugged his thighs, and
the thin white net-style pullover showed glimpses
of six-pack abs.

She rushed over to the breakfast buffet and
poured a glass of cranberry juice. Stuart Lowell
was not the man she should be looking at in
this manner. She couldn't understand it. Most
of the female side of the Godfreys and Lowells
thought he was "to die for" in a tux. Why had
a pair of tight jeans done the same thing for
her?

Later that morning, they dropped off Tyler
and Jolene at the airport, then drove up to Sag
Harbor. The backseat held their luggage while
the spacious trunk and rooftop rack held the
boxes they would need. Danita had no problem
with Stuart driving. She took the time to review
some plans and then fell asleep. She awoke at
about three in the afternoon just as they entered Captain's Row. Tyler and Mary had purchased the mansion early in their marriage,
when they planned on having several children.

As they drove up, Danita was again impressed with the house. They just didn't make houses like that anymore. The four large bedrooms, master suite, and library all had ten-foot ceilings. There was a wine cellar and a very private pool.

For more than three decades this had been a well-used house. It was great for entertaining, especially in the warm weather. Stuart spent summer vacations here. When the serene house had been a haven for Danita and her mother, she wasn't friendly with the kids who lived in Sag Harbor. She was happy just to play in the yard, swim a bit, and even take the short walk to the town's shops. It was here that she decided to study hard and be successful. She knew a business degree would get her a vice presidency of Lowell's. She'd heard about the stores all her life. Until then she'd been content to explore her options. After her father left, she was determined to take his place, and she let nothing get in her way. Not even love.

"I guess we'll take our old rooms," Stuart said. "You liked the view of the pool and I liked the view of the street. You know, one day you're going to have to let all that frustration out."

"What frustration?"

"You're feelings about your father."

"We are here to take care of things for Tyler, not to discuss my father," she said through clenched teeth.

"Well, you mumbled a lot about him while you were sleeping. . . ."

"Why didn't you just wake me up, or were you too interested in what I was saying?"

"Look, I don't care if you never talk to me about it. But talk to someone. You need to get it out of your system."

"For your information, unlike you, I got it out of my system a long time ago. Let's get inside."

"What do you mean, unlike me?" Stuart asked.

"Sorry, I shouldn't have said that"

"I want an answer." The tone was quiet but lethal.

"Gossip. I heard that your ex still expects you to take care of her."

"It's not gossip. It's true. But I'll know when to stop. You see, Nikki is seeing a director, and when they get married, my alimony payments will be over. Of course, she thinks I don't know this. I know something else. If I resist, she'll always be there."

"It seems to me that it would be the other way around. If you give her money, she'll always be there."

"Nikki thinks that same way, but once she marries this guy, I'm a free man."

"I think you're wrong."

"You don't know Nikki."

"So, is that what you're trying to do with me? Play analyst? Well, stop. You will never know me well enough to do that."

"Whatever you say."

Stuart popped the trunk, and by the time he got out and walked to the back of the car, Danita was dragging her luggage out. Stuart took his luggage and with long strides reached the door at the same time she did. He unlocked the door and they went in. She went right to the bedroom she'd stayed in as a child and closed the door. She was angry but not with Stuart. She knew he was right. She also knew that if the anger at her father disappeared, she might lose her ambition also. She couldn't let that happen until after Tyler's decision. She even knew what she'd ask for if she didn't get the promotion. She would ask for six months off and she would spend the first month in Paris, finding out more from her father. Then she would go away and let all her demons fade, but for now she needed those demons.

More than fifteen minutes had passed before she returned to the living room. Stuart had made himself at home and was nursing a glass of wine. He held up his glass. "Want one?"

"Yes. Thank you."

"I'm sorry. . . ."

"I apologize. . . ."

They spoke simultaneously, then laughed. "I'm not saying you're wrong," Danita told him. "But I just can't discuss my father with you."

He poured a glass of chardonnay and handed it to her. Their hands touched, and some of the wine spilled over on her hand. Without thinking, she ran her tongue across her thumb and licked the wine. Stuart knew she didn't realize how sensuous that small act was. His eyes met hers and held them for longer than necessary, and then he stepped away.

They had found common ground. She had given him the boundaries of this relationship, and since they were going to be in close quarters for the next three weeks, this was a relationship. As he watched her walk over to a plush chair, he noticed she was thin but not skinny. The white leggings hugged her small frame, emphasizing all the right curves. He hadn't noticed that this morning. Why now? The last thing he needed was to feel anything more than brotherly love. But they weren't related, and he hoped she had a pair of jeans to work in.

"Yes, I do."

"You do what?"

"Have a pair of jeans to work in. That was what you asked, wasn't it?"

"Oh, uh . . . yes . . . I was just thinking that white would get dirty too fast."

After dinner, Danita pulled out her trusty legal pad and a pen as they decided what to tackle first. They both agreed to begin with the hardest job and work to easy. That meant the first thing they would tackle was the library.

"We need a keeper room. A place to put the things that we know will be taken to the Manhattan place."

"Let's use the kitchen. There's less to move

around, and we aren't going to do that much in the kitchen. Jolene stocked a lot of microwave stuff," Stuart said. He'd checked that right away.

"Then we'll use the breakfast nook. It's pretty large."

"Tyler gave me the keys to his brownstone, so we might rent a U-Haul and take some things down. It would give us a chance to do something in the city."

"Like?"

"A Broadway show?"

"Sounds great, but I don't want to spend more time here than I have to."

"I agree."

Three

When Stuart woke the next morning, he felt good, but there was something missing. He had a very rigorous physical training session each morning in California before he went to work. After all, living in Malibu, he couldn't sell to the "pretty people" and be out of shape. He tried to jog a lot, but he really liked working out in a gym. He liked the idea of pushing himself until he went to the next level. It was too bad the house didn't have a weight room.

It didn't seem to matter that he had this assignment, which should have taken the place of his normal push. If he started feeling out of it, he would just begin a jogging program.

Stuart was thinking how he needed to keep the boutique fun and interesting, and that was getting difficult. Dax had given him a few hints, and he used them successfully, but Stuart knew that he was moving away from the younger crowd. He was thirty-two and for women in Hollywood, that was over the hill, so he was constantly searching for the next best thing. He was

a little tired of new and he liked traditional.
That's why he wanted New York. It catered to
both new and traditional and it was a challenge
to please both.

He'd bought the beach house after his divorce, and he loved it, but he was getting tired
of living there every day. He would always keep
it for vacations, but he wanted to live in a high-
rise with a doorman in a city where he could
walk around or take mass transit so he wouldn't
really need a car. Stuart was convinced his de-
parture would also help Dax. It was time his
brother stopped being a playboy.

Nikki claimed he bought the beach house out
of spite because he knew she wanted to live at
the beach, but he was too involved then with
Lowell's, which was having some growing pains,
to think of a house purchase. His Malibu staff
was fun—bright and hard working—and he
wanted to keep that kind of laid-back camara-
derie that he thought was right for Dax's personality. Stuart wanted to take on New York.

He didn't like closing up this Sag Harbor
house, but not for the same reason that Danita
didn't want to. For Stuart it was just plain bor-
ing. He'd taken very little when he and Nikki
broke up. He'd packed his clothes, music, and
video collection. Since they had such diverse
tastes, she was happy to get rid of things.

He got up and did a few push-ups and sit-ups
and then he showered, dressed in khakis and a
T-shirt, and went to the kitchen. He felt a little

better when he learned that Danita was still asleep. He fixed an omelet and coffee for himself and put water to boil for tea.

He felt rather than heard her when she joined him. He was surprised at how beautiful she looked in the morning. Her pixie face glowed, and she seemed as if she had gotten more rest than he did.

Danita wore jeans and a shirt that allowed her to move freely. He didn't realize how much he was scrutinizing her until she called his name.

"You seemed to be in another world. I've asked you twice where I can find an omelet pan. They used to be on this side, but I see things have been rearranged."

"Sorry. They're in the top cabinet. I'll get it." He stood up and pulled down another omelet pan for her.

Tyler had a cleaning crew come in and make the house tidy before he corralled Stuart and Danita to do the rest of the work.

She glanced at the pan in the kitchen sink. "You didn't use the right oil."

"And?"

"And that's why most of your omelet is still in the pan."

Danita gave him a quick lesson in how to have more egg on your plate than in the pan. "You should get some of that nonstick spray. It's healthier than oil anyway."

He watched her as she hit her rhythm and prepared a beautiful omelet. She surprised him by slipping it onto his plate and then began to prepare one for herself.

Stuart picked up a fork and tasted it. He knew it looked good, but how did it taste?

"Terrific. Where did you learn to cook?"

"Here. Mom and I were living here for a while, and we did a lot of things. Did you know that she designed the garden in the back?"

"I think Tyler mentioned it a couple of times."

"What's on the agenda for today?"

"Let's finish the library. Then I'll start with the bedrooms upstairs, and we'll work our way down."

"Okay. Did Tyler mention what he wanted to do with the furniture?"

"No. We'll just pack the easy-to-move items and then talk to him."

He pushed the hot water closer to her. She poured herself a cup of tea, then covered it with the saucer and let it steep.

She was eating her omelet, when she felt his eyes on her. "What's the matter?"

"Nothing. I just enjoy seeing this version of you."

"This version?"

"Softer. More accessible."

"Can't be the boss and be too soft."

"Do you really have to be the boss?"

"What's that supposed to mean?" Her eyes narrowed, and cold shards dripped from every word.

"Don't get crazy on me. I'm just asking if you and Chris work together, or do you give him a chance to be boss even when you're in the office."

She knew she didn't. She'd never thought about letting Chris run things when she was there. "Do you do that with your people?"

"Sure. Try it sometime."

Danita took her cup of tea and went into the library. It was her way of blocking him out and not letting him tell her how to lead her crew. She knew he might be right. She also knew that since she'd been at the Sag Harbor house, she hadn't needed any of the antacids she usually took to get through the day. She was sleeping better, and she liked it.

Stuart gave her a few moments and then came in and started to work on the bookshelves. Danita watched the muscles in his back ripple when he reached upward and pulled the books to the floor.

Danita sipped her tea and gazed out the library window. Despite all her attempts to prevent it, a tear rolled down her cheek.

He'd been so sure she was thinking about how she ran her store that he didn't look at her until he'd cleaned off the shelf. Then he saw she was crying.

"Hey, I'm sorry. I didn't mean to upset you."

"You didn't. I'm upset because I love this

house and I can't believe Tyler is going to sell
it."

Stuart knew what she meant. He remembered
the good times in this house. He just wasn't as
attached to it as she was. "Why don't you buy
it?"

"When would I use it?"

"You'd find time. I'm going to check the
space in the breakfast nook again. I think we
can get everything in there."

"I'll start packing the boxes." She put the
cup down and pulled a box near the books. As
she worked, she wondered if Stuart was right. If
she bought the house from Tyler and didn't get
the New York store, could she find enough time
to use it? She wasn't sure. She would talk to her
uncle about keeping the house off the market
until she knew.

Right then she could concentrate on only one
goal at a time for herself. That goal was Tyler's
seat on the board. Once that was settled, she
could think about everything else.

Stuart returned and carried one of the boxes
to the breakfast nook. That's how they continued to work. He seemed to appear as soon as
she finished packing a box and whisked it away.
By two-thirty the library had been cleared of
books.

When he came back from taking out the last
box of books, he said, "Let's get out of here
for a while."

Again they showered and changed clothes.

Danita chose a black shirtdress, since the button-down front gave an illusion of height. She'd lost a few pounds and was afraid she looked sickly rather than petite. She added a light dusting of powder and a maroon lipstick that seemed to give her skin a better color. Then she slipped into black, leather high-heeled sandals. As with most women under 5'4", she'd worn heels for so long, she wasn't comfortable in flat shoes.

They decided against walking into town and opted for driving to a restaurant. They cruised around until they found a restaurant that offered salads and fresh seafood and stopped there.

As they ate, they talked about how they would finish the project. "I think we can clear out everything that can be moved," Stuart said.

"Then we can take an inventory of what's left, and then we're finished."

"I think we tried to do too much today."

Danita laughed. "We want to get it over with and get back to our real lives."

"I thought you just wanted to get away from me."

She looked at him. "Maybe. We weren't exactly getting along."

"Why is that?"

"I . . . guess we know we want the same thing."

"Did you ever think we could share the store?"

"Share?"

"Work together?"

"How could we do that? Tyler is a board member, and there's room for only one."

"Right."

There was no room for compromise. It was an either/or situation, and that would never change. Stuart knew Danita felt the same way. They couldn't share it. It could belong to only one of them.

"I wonder what's happening with Tyler and Dax," Danita said to change the subject.

"Can you imagine being a fly on the wall?"

"I hope Dax goes back to using his talent."

"He might leave the country."

"If it's what he really wants, I don't care."

They drove back to the house and had time to box up the lamps and knickknacks from the library. They moved the furniture against the wall, and suddenly the library was bare. One room down and seven to go.

"I used to be intimidated by this room," Danita said.

"I can't believe that."

"Don't get me wrong. I loved the library, but I couldn't imagine how you could gather all those books in one room. The ceilings were so high. Remember how you needed a chair to get the books off the top shelf?"

He nodded. "They used to put the R-rated

Viveca Carlysle

her hair in her face. She thought back about how she enjoyed Stuart's kiss. What was wrong ...th having an affair with him? How about the ... ...ach other? She'd r...d

stuff up there, and I used to get the books down for them."

"Shame on you."

"I was discreet. They had to be mature enough to see it."

"And you decided who was mature enough?"

"Of course."

"Did you ever get caught?"

"Oh, yes."

"So what happened?"

"My father took me behind closed doors and explained why I shouldn't get the books down, and to make sure I understood, he introduced me to the business end of his belt."

"How old were you?"

"Twelve. I went on the sunporch and got the ladder."

Danita shook her head and burst into laughter. "You were always a little devil."

"I guess so. What was it that made you like that library so much?"

"I found a book called *Scruples* by Judith Krantz. It was about a fabulous store."

"So you wanted to re-create the store in the book?"

"Not really. I wanted to re-create the same feeling. A store that makes you want to shop only there."

"Then I started looking for other books that would give me that feeling."

She looked so innocent. Her eyes had a faraway look. He leaned forward, and before he realized it, he'd kissed her. But the light kiss wasn't enough. He pulled her closer and the kiss became bolder and bolder, until she pushed him away. "What's the matter with you?"

Now he couldn't move. He hadn't meant to kiss her, but he couldn't stop himself. It was one of the rare times he lost control.

"You just look so soft and pure."

"Well . . ."

"Why not?"

"We don't even like each other."

"Maybe we do."

He leaned forward and kissed her again. This time she took another approach. She didn't move. No pushing, she just froze him out.

"I guess you're right. You don't like me," Stuart said after the kiss.

"Why is it when I feel I can trust you, the next thing you do makes me think you're a jerk?"

"It won't happen again," he promised.

She watched Stuart back up until he reached the archway between the library and the hallway, and then he turned. Danita didn't move until she heard the front door open and close.

She walked to the mirror in the hallway and stared at herself. She ran her fingers across her mouth. She had enjoyed his kiss, and it frightened her. How could she? He was the enemy. Just as she told him, they didn't like each other. Her friends all talked about toe-curling kisses, but she had never experienced one until then.

She didn't look any different, but she certain. felt different.

She ran to her room, got a jacket and sli... on her loafers. She did... house alo...

ee, and slipped
n't want to be in the
ne. She walked to town, then down
Main Street, and acted as if she were studying
the different houses. Sag Harbor did have interesting architecture. She took a leisurely stroll
and timed herself. She walked in one direction
for about half an hour and then turned around
and walked back. It helped her relax. She felt
the tension release, tension she didn't know existed.

But for the past year she did have that knot
in her stomach, evidence that something was
wrong, and although she hated doctors, the
knot had scared her enough to see one. She
was happy to learn that it was from stress, but
the doctor warned her that she was coming dan-
gerously close to developing an ulcer. When she
arrived at Sag Harbor, she didn't have to take
her trusty antacid, but once Stuart kissed her,
the knot returned. The physical activity of packing up the house was probably the best thing
for her. It kept her from punching his face.

Her original plan went out the window. She
kept walking until she reached the sea. By that
time she was tired and sat on a boulder to rest
before starting back.

The temperature was dropping, and she felt
the breeze getting stronger, and since she had
not taken a hat or scarf, the wind was blowing

fact that they didn't like each other. She'd read an article about having "lust in your heart," and maybe that was why she couldn't maintain the anger.

She'd never developed a legitimate crush on Stuart when they were growing up, but a couple of her cousins had. They were shattered when he married Nikki. They didn't like her because she thought she should be waited on by all the Godfreys and the Lowells, but Danita found something else wrong with the woman. Nikki never complimented a woman without insulting her. Her favorite target was Skye.

"That color blue looks so good on you," Nikki had said, "You looked like a blimp in that yellow you wore yesterday."

Danita knew from the way Nikki's eyes narrowed after she'd throw out these little zingers that the woman got pleasure out of finding a vulnerable spot and upsetting someone.

Of course, she was the complete femme fatale as far as the men were concerned. She made sure they never heard her say anything hurtful. They saw her as a beautiful, gracious woman. Danita wondered how long it would be before she showed her true self to Stuart. The marriage hadn't lasted too long.

Danita tried to pay more attention to her surroundings and less to Stuart. Unfortunately, she made that decision just as she passed a young couple who were oblivious of her and were locked in an embrace.

She had had only one serious relationship. When she was in college she'd met a man who pretended he didn't know her family. He courted her in an old-fashioned way that made her think they were headed for marriage. As soon as she slept with him, he pushed for meetings with her family, asked if she knew of a company that might be looking for go-getters, and then turned nasty when she suggested firms other than her family's. When she explained that there were only a few executive positions in Lowell's for outsiders, he stopped calling within days. What she did after that affair was make it clear to anyone she dated who she was and that she didn't run an employment agency.

A drop of rain fell on Danita, and she stood. She walked quickly back to the house and arrived just as the sprinkles became drops.

Stuart was standing in the front yard. "Where have you been?"

"I went for a walk. What's the matter, did you think I ran away over a little kiss."

"I thought it was possible."

"Don't flatter yourself."

"I'm not. It was wrong."

"Well, since we both agree, we can forget it and start over."

He didn't want to forget it. He wanted to kiss her again.

"Thank you."

Just as they closed the door, there was a large clap of thunder, and the rain poured down as if the sky had broken open.

"Hope there's something in the pantry that's pretty easy to fix," he said.

"Me too. There's no way we can go out tonight."

The house had central heating, but it also had seven fireplaces. Danita said she'd fix dinner if he'd start the fire.

"And the next time it rains, you fix dinner and I'll start the fire."

"Only if there are lots of TV dinners in that refrigerator."

They laughed about their meager talents, and that helped them talk about something other than that kiss.

They got down to their individual chores. Danita decided on an old-fashioned steak-and-potatoes meal. The built-in grill was state-of-the-art. Dinner was ready in an hour, and they used the large coffee table to hold the meal and sat cross-legged on the floor as they ate.

Their conversation centered around safe subjects until they were cleaning the kitchen and Stuart asked where he stood with her.

Danita knew he was watching her. The heat began to rise in her face.

"If I ask you a straight question, will you answer it?" Stuart said.

"Mmm . . . yes."

"We like the same things, we want to work in the same place. Did you ever wonder if we could be more than just friends?"

"I—I didn't, but some of my cousins were thinking of hara-kiri when you got married."

"Did they celebrate when we broke up?"

"No. Alas, by the time you were available, they had outgrown the crush."

"What about *you?*"

Danita hesitated long enough to take a sip of water. "Why pursue it? We don't like each other."

"We don't have to like each other to be attracted to each other."

"But I would have to like you to do anything about it. Men don't seem to have that problem. I can't understand it."

"Procreation and sex is what makes the world go around."

"I'm not interested in making the world go around. I'm interested in someone who will give to me as much as I give to him. And anyway, what about those starlets who hang all over you?"

"I'm kind of a safe date for them. Those women are so ambitious, they don't have room in their lives for romance. I'm not looking for

romance either so it's pretty nice. I get to go
to a lot of premieres, the stores get free publicity, and no one gets hurt."

"Do they call you, or is it like a regular
date?"

"Both. If I'm going to something that will be
in the newspapers or on TV, I might call one
of these ladies."

"But you married Nikki."

Stuart was quiet for so long, Danita turned to
see if he heard her. "I'll tell you all about Nikki
when you can tell me all about your dad."

For Danita, that meant she would never know
anything more than she had gathered through
the gossip mill.

Stuart suggested they watch a video tape, and
they were surprised that Tyler's collection was
so up-to-date. They also realized how many movies they hadn't seen.

They decided on an action-adventure movie
that allowed them to get lost in the characters.
After the movie, they worked on a game plan
for the next day. The minor skirmish over the
kiss had set them back, but they would make it
up. They couldn't let that happen again.

That night Danita slept fitfully. Sharp, jag-
ged visions danced through her head. She
woke up several times during the night. She
knew it was because she wanted someone to
talk to, but there was no one she could
trust, to tell about her father. She knew that
someday she would have to talk about it, but

Stuart Lowell had been her enemy for too long, and she wasn't sure of the olive branch he was extending.

Four

Pain. Sharp, piercing pain woke her up. It felt like severe heartburn, and she tried to remember what she'd eaten to cause it. She ran her hand over her abdomen just under her breastbone. She tried to get to her antacid tablets but couldn't find them. She dragged herself to the bathroom and washed her face. Her thin gown was soaked with sweat, so she slipped it off. She had remembered to buy a nightgown but had forgotten to bring a robe.

What could hurt so much? She was suddenly afraid and grateful she wasn't alone. She couldn't take it anymore. She needed help. Slowly, she crept along the wall, holding on to each piece of furniture as she made her way to the door. The distance between her room and Stuart's was no more than fifteen feet, but it seemed more like a mile. She tried to call out to him. But her voice was raspy and her throat dry.

She stumbled into the table in the hall, and the lamp crashed to the floor. The door to Stuart's room opened. He stood there a moment, absorbing the frail woman holding on to the table. He rushed to her and she collapsed in his arms.

"What's wrong?"

"Sick. Stomach hurts."

He lowered her to the floor and rushed to her bedroom. He couldn't find a robe, so he grabbed her purse. It flittered through his mind that Lowell's had a terrific medical plan.

Returning to her, he asked her to sit still while he got dressed, which he did in record time. He put his robe around her and ushered her out to the car. In minutes they were on their way to the hospital.

It had been a shock to his system seeing her like that. She'd been his sparring partner too long. What if it were her appendix? What if it burst before she made it to the hospital? He checked her out of the corner of his eye. Her eyes were closed. Her long lashes were dark and stood out against her skin, which was now more yellow than golden. What would he tell her mother if this was serious?

The pain had eased by the time they got to the emergency room, and she was able to walk into the hospital, albeit very slowly.

While she was examined, Stuart paced the waiting room floor.

Hospitals made him nervous and Stuart decided to take a short walk. Just a short distance from the hospital he saw a man entering a small shop. Within minutes he'd convinced the man to let him buy a robe for Danita. He knew she'd feel more comfortable in something that fit. Stuart returned to the hospital just in time to meet her doctor. He was an elderly, slightly stooped man who looked like an absentminded professor.

"Are you her husband?"

"No, but we're family."

A moment later, Danita joined them. She was weak but tried to smile. "I guess I scared you a little."

"She's going to be fine, but she's got to take better care of herself."

"Was it food poisoning?"

"No." The doctor looked at Danita, and she nodded, giving him permission to discuss with Stuart what he'd already told her. "This young woman has the subtle beginnings of an ulcer."

"She's too young for that."

The doctor chuckled. "There is no such thing as too young. I see your type all the time. Long hours, erratic eating, you just don't think long-term."

"What should she do?"

"Milk helps, but she should get rid of whatever is causing the stress."

When they finished speaking with the doctor, he bundled her up in the car again and they drove slowly through the night.

"What's going on with you?"

"Nerves. I had this in college. Just before exams I was close to a breakdown." She would never let Stuart know the truth.

"You graduated magna cum laude."

"Sure, but I thought I was going to fail every time I took a test. I drove my roommate crazy. She would be calm and just hope for a passing grade, and I was afraid if I got less than ninety on the test, the professor would fail me."

"That isn't rational."

"I wasn't rational at the time."

The closer they got to the house, the quieter Danita became. She was revealing more about herself to this man than she ever had to anyone. Even in school, when she found a friend she had a lot in common with, she didn't talk about what it was like to be part of this huge family, what the pressure to succeed was like. No one who wasn't going through it would be able to understand it.

Once in the house, he helped her to her room and into bed. "Are you going to be okay?"

"Sure. I'm beginning to feel like my old self again."

"Well, you're going to take it easy for a couple of days. I don't want Tyler coming down on me for not taking care of you."

Stuart lay on his bed that night, afraid to close his eyes in case she needed him again. He stared at the ceiling. He was in a strange predicament. He'd wanted the New York store to prove he could succeed on both coasts. Until recently, he hadn't known about Danita wanting it. Now he couldn't drop out. If he did, Danita would not be grateful. She wanted to get the store on her own merit. But he wasn't sure she was the right person for the job, and he was concerned about her health.

The next day, Stuart insisted that Danita stay in bed, and since she hadn't slept well, she took his advice. She lay in bed and wondered what would happen when "the cousins" found out about New York.

There were some who would say certain family members were interested in a position just to annoy the person who wanted it. That had happened when Danita took over D.C. The most vocal was Morgan Sylvester. He'd married Skye Godfrey because he thought that was easy access to the top positions. He was sorely disappointed when he learned that there was no way he'd make it to the top.

He made a lot of noise about it, but eventually he settled down and worked on his store in Atlanta. Since then he'd grumbled to anyone who listened to how he felt he'd been taken for a ride.

Of course, word got back to Alan Lowell, Stuart's father, and Morgan was summoned to Virginia. After a couple of days with Alan, Morgan had changed his tune and was doing quite well in Lowell's GA.

Although she and Stuart had come to a truce, that didn't mean times would be easy. They were the future of Lowell's, and they knew it. They also knew that they were rivals. How successful their store was determined their standing in the corporation. Tyler Godfrey was the kingpin of the group, and Stuart's father was next in line. Some thought he could rule everything if he ever opted to leave his Virginia estate and take up residence in New York.

That wasn't to say that Tyler was not a shrewd businessman. He held his own with any of the current men who appeared in *Fortune* magazine or made the Forbes top-entrepreneur list. It's just that Tyler sometimes let his heart make decisions for him. Alan never did.

Danita sat on the sofa, sipping milk, while Stuart talked on the phone with his father.

"I know I never take vacations. That's going to change. Dax is doing a great job. Don't worry."

They spoke for a few minutes more before they ended the call.

"What is it with your father?"

"Nothing. He just hates to travel and Tyler loves to."

"I meant the challenges."

Stuart stiffened. "We aren't supposed to talk about that."

"We aren't supposed to talk about it with anyone who doesn't understand it."

"I guess it's tantamount to being called on the carpet by your boss. He finds a mistake, challenges you, and sees if you crack under pressure."

"It's brutal."

"I've been on the receiving end."

"I haven't."

"I know, but you gave him the scenario he wanted to hear."

Yes, Danita remembered, but it wasn't fun or educational, it was just cruel.

At each summit meeting Alan Lowell would challenge a decision made by one of the cousins, and then have another cousin relate what they would have done in such a situation. He'd stop the ritual when he found a plan he liked.

The worst part of that kind of challenge was that each store was listed on a board, ranked by sales. If you lost the challenge, your store was put on the bottom, no matter how good your sales were.

The best part was that it was never done outside the dining room of Alan's estate, so only the cousins knew your fate. Since it could happen to any of them, they never talked about it.

Danita dreaded the moment when it would be her turn to get challenged. It hadn't happened in three years.

At the last summit meeting she attended, Alan challenged the annual report of Lowell's FL and the way Nick Lowell handled an embarrassing situation. It seems that a visiting movie star's credit card was declined and the young clerk said there was nothing he could do. The woman began ranting and raving until Nick settled the matter by allowing the sale, based on the woman's assurance that it was a mistake.

To pacify her, he also allowed her to select a dress for an award show and accepted a check. A few days later the check bounced and the woman declared bankruptcy.

"How would you handle it?" Alan turned to Danita.

"Get the woman off the floor and into an office. Then check with the credit card company again. Confront her with the facts. Then give her an option. She could leave the store carrying an empty box so people would think that everything was fine."

"Now, there's a woman who can think on her feet."

Nick jumped up. "So people would think that we got taken anyway."

"No," said Danita. "After she declared bankruptcy, just admit the charge hadn't gone through, but out of respect for her, everything in the box was a gift. We look good and we told the truth." Nick and Danita had never been close and now never would be.

Nick was furious as Tyler put the Florida store at the bottom of the ranking. Danita wondered how many of the other vice presidents suffered from the same kind of stomach trouble she experienced.

Later she tried to talk to Nick, but he was still livid. "You don't know what it's like in my store," he almost growled at her. It would be hours before he calmed down and they could talk about things besides work.

From that time on, if she could avoid the meetings, she did. The cousins were always competing. They didn't know how to have uninhibited, traditional fun.

Stuart had not escaped his father's wrath. In her first year at this annual bloodletting, she had watched Alan knock down every idea Stuart had for changes in the California store.

"Alan attacks too hard and too often."

"I guess it's the theory that 'what doesn't destroy me makes me stronger.'"

"I think he should stop doing it."

There was a board in Alan's office that showed the stores and the executive in charge. Danita in D.C., Nick in Florida, Stuart in California, Sheila in Massachusetts, Gemma in Hawaii, Marcus in Ohio, Brandon in New Mexico, Morgan in Georgia, Tyler in New York, and Roberta in Dallas.

They had been portrayed in the media as upstanding, hardworking owners of one of the few family-owned businesses. The image was becoming too hard to live up to. Dax had rebelled, but once Tyler pulled Stuart away, it seemed that even the most rebellious of the group could be brought in line.

When the scandal broke regarding Danita's father, his younger brother was given the job, and for sixteen years Tyler had proved to be successful.

Now that he wanted to step down, his position was opened to the cousins, but they weren't jumping through hoops to get it. Most felt that the competition was between Stuart and Danita and were content to see the result.

Most were surprised to hear that Stuart would actually go after the position. The California stores were a feather in his cap. There was no need for him to prove he was good. Rumor said that Alan had pushed him into the ring because he didn't want a woman running the landmark store.

Even though people didn't know about the little challenges Alan liked, he was considered a tough, ruthless competitor. Both Stuart and Danita had grown up thinking he was gruff but family. He'd never been other than kind to her or her mother. After Stuart's mother passed away, only Elizabeth, Danita's mother, could talk to him. They were the best of friends.

As Danita thought about her family, she wondered if Alan had ever torn her father apart. If he'd made him cringe during a review session. She wondered if any one of the Godfreys or Lowells could ever live a normal life.

Knowing that Stuart was downstairs working while she relaxed made her feel a little guilty. It was as if she were getting her payback for all the times he came out as the star of the family and she was only second best.

She was proud of what she'd done in D.C., but Stuart had been given a chance and had created an entirely new source of income for the family with the Malibu boutique, a younger, hipper version of the main store. She had so many special-event ideas but her favorite had been the etiquette lessons, and while they flourished, they weren't to be compared to the boutique.

Danita had always avoided being near Stuart. She was grateful for his help the night before, but why couldn't he be happy with California? If her father hadn't been forced to leave, he would have been running the flagship store, and it would have been hers by default. Sometimes life wasn't fair.

She stared at the ceiling and fought back the frustration over not being able to do something special that all the family would be proud of. Somehow she thought she could do that with the New York store. It didn't matter that she'd had success in D.C. Yes, it was the nation's capital and yes, she'd done most of it by herself. But she still felt that she hadn't done enough.

There was a soft knock on the door. Danita called for Stuart to enter.

"Well, you certainly look better than you did last night," he said. "I'll fix you a tray."

"Don't. If I stay in this room any longer, I'm going to go crazy."

"Good. I hate eating alone when I don't have to."

"Then let's watch a movie."

* * *

The relocation to the den required a bit of teamwork. Danita wanted to have her notes for the charity event and her laptop.

Danita had used an illusionist for a special event in D.C. She had always been fascinated with magic and she'd wanted to invite him back but this event in New York would be a showcase for him and for her.

She knew the illusionist was available and she was excited about being able to give him a larger forum for his work. Besides, she wanted to see the act again to see if she could uncover his secrets.

When she was finally settled in, Stuart brought her dinner. He handed her a tray with soup, crackers, and a glass of milk. "The doctor said not eat anything heavy for a couple of days."

"You didn't have to do this. . . ."

"It's okay. I hope it makes up for my bumbling around last night."

"You did everything right last night. I was the one who was a little crazy. How's the project coming?"

"You know what a ringer is?" he asked.

"You mean someone who is slipped into a contest who probably has all the answers?"

"Exactly."

"That's what Tyler is."

"I don't understand."

"Someone's been through here before. All the good stuff is packed away in the basement. The only thing left was the library. We were set up."

"Why?"

"Who knows? Maybe Tyler thinks that we'll work out our differences or kill each other and then he can give the New York store to someone else." She laughed after she said that.

"So?" He raised an eyebrow.

"Well, they were right. As soon as we started working together, we found some common ground."

"While I was moving boxes, I tried to remember my last vacation."

"When was that?"

"I think I was three."

They laughed, but she felt an underlying pain. Was it true? Was work all they ever did?

The movie they chose this time was a suspense thriller. Neither of them had seen it when it was released, so they began to challenge each other as to the ending. Who would figure it all out first?

"That may not work for us. I watched a show once where the detective went to the theater to see a play and made a guess who the killer was. He was wrong, but what upset him the most was that there was a clue that wasn't shown to the audience."

"That's cheating," Danita said.

"That's what he said."

They worked through the plot and dialogue. They were doing great until the detective uncovered the killer and they were shocked they had misread all the clues.

"That's worse than having a clue withheld. They gave us all the clues we needed and we were still wrong."

"I guess we'd better stick to running a store," Stuart laughed.

After the film, they remained seated comfortably on the sofa. "What do you daydream about, Danita?" Stuart asked.

She knew exactly what he was saying. "I dream about being successful and admired and that my store has the best bottom line."

"Don't you find that strange?"

"Yes. I know I should want a home and family, but it's—I need to do this first."

"What about that biological clock women are always talking about?"

"I don't think I have one."

For the first time in her life, Danita had said out loud what she had been thinking for years. At the summit meetings, she avoided the children who were there. She didn't rush to hold the new babies. She didn't marvel over the growth spurts of the others. She preferred the older children.

The last time, her cousin Skye's four-year-old put glue in her three-year-old sister's hair. One of the other children thought he had super powers and tried to jump from the swing to the slide and knocked out a tooth.

In her head, she knew these incidents were few and far between, but it bothered her that she felt so helpless around children.

"Do you want children?" she asked.

"Yeah, I can see these little smiling faces in my mind. Each time they pop into my head, I see myself coming home from work and my wife and kids waiting for me. Dinner is ready, and after the kids are in bed, my wife and I plan our future."

"What does your wife look like?"

"She's tall, slender . . . sometimes she's petite. . . ."

"Does she work?"

"Of course. Maybe she didn't have a career before, but I've changed her mind."

"If you think she didn't have a career before she married you, that's a fantasy."

"No, the fantasy comes after my wife and I are in bed."

Danita shook her finger at him. "I don't think I want to hear about that."

"Okay, let's keep it clean," he said.

"Do you daydream often?"

"No. Most of the time I'm too tired. As soon as I get in the house, I just want to go to sleep. I enjoyed the two stores at first, but now it's a little rough."

"Maybe it will be better now that Dax is on board."

"I'm not holding my breath. I don't think he'll last." He didn't want to reveal any more, so he changed the subject. "What kind of home life do you want?"

"I want a home life that makes me want to leave work early." Her throat suddenly had a knot in it.

"Do you have a picture in your mind?"

"Yes."

"Close your eyes and tell me about it."

She closed her eyes and leaned her head back on the sofa. "I'm driving home but not from work. Maybe from my bridge club. The house is in a quiet neighborhood. It's a single-family house, and so are the others on the block. There are no apartment buildings, no busy streets, no loud music. I pull into the driveway and there's a car already there. It's my husband's. I go inside and he's waiting with a drink. Dinner is ready and waiting."

"Now, *that's* a fantasy."

"Shh, let me finish. We have a housekeeper who does the cooking. She doesn't live in, so by nine, she's gone home. My husband and I sit in the den and kiss. Then it gets X-rated."

"Did you think you'd have that kind of life with the congressman?"

"Yes. I was prepared to walk away from Lowell's if he'd asked me. Can you imagine that? I was going to give up everything for him. He wasn't prepared to give an inch for me. That's when I decided I would never do that again.

The man I marry will have to accept the full package or we can't have a relationship."

Tears leaked from under her lashes. Stuart saw them and understood. He waited until she composed herself.

"I understand."

Her eyes opened. That's what he said about her father, but it wasn't true. His eyes told her that he also had that memory.

"Why did you get so angry that day when I said I understood about your father?"

"Because my father was my hero. I loved him and he was going away. You still had your father, so how could you understand?"

"I thought you were angry because everyone knew what he did."

"That may have been part of it."

"You know, there were times when I wished it had been my father."

"Why?"

"He's a tyrant. He plays the charming southern gentleman to the hilt, but he was not a good father. All those skills he has in taking a person apart he honed on my brother and me. Today that would be called child abuse."

"You and Dax turned out pretty good."

"That's because of my mother. She was the one who created the place we could live and grow in."

"She reminded me of my mom."

"I know."

"I know Alan is tough, but let's face it, how

many black-owned companies fail every year?
Maybe he was just afraid to fail or have you
fail."

"Maybe he wanted to make us fail?"

"If your father was so bad, why did you come
into the company?"

"I still wanted to please him. I wanted him
to be proud of me. After a while, I started enjoying it. Now I can't wait to get to work and
try new ideas."

"I feel the same way. I just get anxious when
things aren't going right."

"The sad thing is that there are so many
brothers out there who would love to be in my
position."

"I've had little girls say they want to grow up
and be just like me. It takes everything in me
not to scream 'no, you don't want my life,' but
of course I just smile and thank them."

"When do you daydream?"

"I try not to. Maybe just before I fall asleep
I might think about another lifestyle, but when
I'm awake, the only thing on my mind is the
store."

"It's good to daydream once in a while."

"What good does it do to daydream?" She
flung the words at him. "We aren't going to
have dreams of our own. We have only the ones
that our families give us. Do you know when I
was in fifth grade, the teacher asked what I
wanted to be when I grew up. I said, 'Vice president.' She thought I was talking about the vice

president of the United States. I was talking about Lowell's."

Both understood that having a family business was a mixed blessing. It gave them a head start in the working world, but it stopped them from ever knowing if they wanted something else.

Five

Counting sheep was not working, and Danita was growing more frustrated. She glanced at the clock on her night table. Only fifteen minutes had passed and now it was four-twenty A.M. She should have been able to sleep through the night after all she had experienced. Most of the time she could almost will herself to fall asleep.

She knew that if she didn't get enough sleep, it would show on her face and Stuart would be concerned about her. After another few minutes she gave up on sleep. If she couldn't sleep, she could work. She slipped out of bed and went into the adjoining bathroom. Her face was a little puffy but nothing she couldn't deal with. She tossed her nightgown in the hamper and turned on the shower. It was refreshing and now she was fully awake.

Nothing could keep her from working on the charity event, no matter how she felt. She wanted to find some other ideas to add to the event. Danita wanted to have a perfect event to introduce herself to New York.

She found something comfortable to put on and got her briefcase. She settled at the vanity table Mary had purchased for her. As she studied the plans for a special event, she remembered something she'd done in D.C. a few months earlier.

It might still be in my laptop, she thought as she reached for the computer. A quick search of the hard drive netted zero. That would mean she transferred it to disk and it was filed away. She picked up her notebook and started writing.

When she was satisfied with her ideas, she put the notebook away. It was now nine-thirty and she wanted some tea.

"Are you sure you should be up?" Stuart asked when he met her at the top of the stairs.

"I'm not helpless, and believe me, I'm much better."

He took her arm. "You don't have to do anything if you don't feel well."

She pulled her arm away. "I'm fine. Don't worry about me." She saw that he was wearing running gear.

"Where are you going?"

"My legs are getting a little weak. I'm used to exercise, so I'm going to take a little run."

"I'll start making lists of things in this room." She sat on the sofa and found her pad and pen.

He stared at her and she finally smiled.

"All I'll do is make lists. I promise."

"See you in an hour."

After he left, she called Tyler in California

and told him she wanted to do a magic show.
He agreed and said that Dax was doing well.
Danita felt a little twinge of regret. If Dax failed,
Stuart would have to go back to California and
she would have New York all to herself. As soon
as the thought came to her, she regretted it.
That was so unfair of her. True to her word,
she didn't move from the sofa. Mary Godfrey
had some of the most beautiful mirrors Danita
had ever seen, she thought as she scanned the
room. She couldn't move them, so she indicated
on the pad where they were located and a little
something about each.

Restless after a while, she wandered around
the main floor of the house, then went outside
by the pool. She sat there and remembered how
worried Stuart had been about her. She'd seen
so many sides of the man that she was confused.
What was she going to do about him?

"If you're not feeling well, maybe we should
call this off," he said from behind her.

"No way. I can pull my own weight"

"Okay. If you insist, why don't we go out for
a walk."

"Don't treat me like an invalid."

"I'm not going to work today. Tomorrow it's
every man for himself."

She was so excited about the benefit she was
planning that she wanted to share her ideas
with him.

"I'm going to handle the entertainment por-
tion of the charity benefit."

"How did that come about?"

"I called Tyler. . . ."

"So when I'm not around you make deals with Tyler?" He frowned and his voice was low but deadly. When she thought up the plan, it had never occurred to her he would feel she was doing something behind his back. She had never intended for that to happen.

"It's something I did in D.C. a few months ago."

"So while I'm worried about *your* health, you're still thinking of what's best for your career."

That was enough for Danita. "This is not about you."

"I wonder."

He saw her stiffen as she stared up at him for several moments. He had made grown men tremble when he spoke to them in that manner. It did not have that effect on Danita. Her hazel eyes were flashing as she spoke. "I have been running a store for three years. I have had to answer to no one but a board of directors. It has nothing to do with you. But if you want to declare war over it, go ahead."

She turned away before he could answer. It always hurts to be accused of something you didn't do. Did he really think that she was so unethical?

He didn't try to talk to her right away. She needed space and he gave it to her. When he finally came back out to the pool, she appeared to be meditating. He walked over to her, and her eyes opened.

"I apologize."

"I accept," she said. "But don't try it again."

A slow smile crept across his face. "Yes, ma'am."

Three days later she was back to her old self. Danita knew that their little project was over, but she didn't want to leave her haven. Once they settled the situation over the benefit, they slipped into a routine that brought them close again. All the years they had competed disappeared and they had begun to enjoy the time they spent together.

They were cataloguing the items in the attic, when Stuart asked, "Why haven't you married?"

"No one wants a woman who's a workaholic."

"I understand that. I have the same problem."

How many times had he and Nikki fought over the fact that he was never home? She'd even promised to give up her career if he would cut back on the time he spent at the store.

"Why are we so driven, Stuart? Why can't we give up part of this desire?"

"Because it's all we know."

"When you and Nikki divorced, the cousins said you paid her a lot of money to keep quiet about you and Laura."

"That's half true. I did pay her a lot of money, and it was because of Laura."

"Oh."

"It's not what you think. Laura was the best administrative assistant I've ever seen, much less worked with. She could almost read my mind. Nikki got jealous. The more I said Laura was my assistant, the more she said Laura was my lover."

"You paid the money so she wouldn't mention Laura during the divorce."

"Laura is married. She and her husband are expecting a baby now. She didn't need the trouble and I didn't want the trouble. I finally told her to look for another job. That was when I became more of a workaholic than I already was."

"Did you have a prenuptial agreement?"

"Yes. You know my dad, he wouldn't have let me get married without protecting the family business, so it was a pretty airtight one. I still help Nikki out because I feel sorry for her."

"If I had her face, I wouldn't need anyone to feel sorry for me."

"Why is it women think they have to look like models to be beautiful?"

"Because men break their darn necks tripping over us to get to a model."

"That's not true of all men."

"You should talk."

He put his arm around her and turned to look at her. She could see the fire in his eyes.

Sharing that much of himself had not been easy, she mused. He leaned forward and started to kiss her, but she pushed him away.

She moved away from him. They were treading on thin ice, and they had to stop.

"We can't stay here right now." He sat next to her on the sofa.

"Why not? Why are you so gung ho to get out of the house?"

She was so tiny, it didn't take much effort for him to pull her against him. "Would you like to stay here with me knowing how I feel?"

Stuart held her hand, then gently pressed her against his body, her head resting on his chest. He didn't want to scare her, but she had to know that he found her attractive. She had to know that he wanted her. No Lowell had ever married a Godfrey, but had there ever been an attraction like this?

She looked up and saw the fire in his dark, sensual eyes. She'd seen him angry, calm, and everything in between, but never had she been exposed to the raw sexuality of the man.

She secretly agreed that it was best that they leave the house for a while. Still, she challenged him by not trying to escape his grasp.

If anything was going to happen between them, it would be Danita's decision.

"I don't feel like going out."

"That may be a bad move."

"I don't know. Maybe we need to get whatever this is out of our systems. Even if it never happens again."

"You'd do that. Sleep with me just to 'get it out of your system.' That wouldn't happen."

"Why not?"

"I've been with enough women to know when one is in my blood. The fever would never leave after one time."

"How many would it take?" She knew she was bluffing, but maybe if she acted aggressive, he'd back off and they could get out of there.

"Come on, you feel what's happening as much as I do."

"Then what do you want?"

"You."

She felt frissons of heat and cold shoot up her spine. She pulled away. She didn't know what to do as their torsos touched. She could feel his frame through his clothes. His sex was firm and heavy, and she knew she was in trouble.

He kissed her and then deepened the kiss. Her knees trembled, her breath caught in her throat and she was lost.

Stuart knew what was happening to her. He ran his fingers along her cheek and shifted slightly, laying her on top of him. He then put his arms down by his sides, giving her a last chance to get up and walk away. But Danita didn't move. She turned her face up to his and her hazel eyes met his black ones. He waited. When she still didn't move, he ran his fingers around the neckline of her garment. She was wearing the bathrobe he'd bought her and his fingers slipped easily into the V of the front opening.

He slipped his hand inside and along the gentle swell of one breast, then the other. As if that weren't enough, he kissed her ear, letting his tongue tease her jawline.

"Oh, no."

"What's the matter?" he asked.

"I'm not sure."

He chuckled. "Neither of us is sure. That's what this is all about. We're going to learn."

Her legs felt as if she had no bones in them. She couldn't stand. She turned her head so she could see if he was real, and she froze.

He felt the change in her body. He swore under his breath. He knew she had allowed reality to interfere with whatever was about to happen. Stuart shifted his weight and moved her back to the sofa.

"I'm sorry." In all her dating life she had never allowed things to go this far, then stopped. She didn't want him to think she was leading him on. She would never do that.

"What happened?"

"I . . . don't love you." Suddenly, as she uttered the words, she knew they weren't true.

"Most people don't have to be in love."

"I do."

He took several deep breaths. "I want you and you want me, so what's the big deal?"

"I thought I could, but I know what will happen when I wake up tomorrow morning. I'll regret it and be angry, and then we'll both be sorry. If it happens. It changes too many things."

"Change can be good."

"Not for us. We're competitors."

"What's that supposed to mean? Will you sleep with me after Tyler makes his decision? Is that want you're saying?"

"No!" She moved to the opposite side of the attic.

"Then how do you decide who you'll sleep with and who you won't?"

She pulled her robe tighter.

"I think my original idea was on target. We've got to get out of this house."

"I brought only clothes that I can work in."

"We'll go someplace casual."

He was *GQ* and she was L.L. Bean. She would have to find something else to wear. As much as she didn't want to go out, she was more afraid of staying in. Each time they clashed, they'd come closer to sharing a bed. Even then, after they'd called a stop to what was happening, she wasn't sure if he kissed her right then, she could stop again.

He got up and walked to the door. "I'm going to wait outside."

She nodded.

"You didn't bring one dress?" Stuart asked. Danita looked at what he was wearing. The cas-

ual slacks and shirt would be appropriate in a
better restaurant.

She went to her room and looked in her
closet. She'd lied. The one thing her mother
always told her was to take a sexy dress and
shoes even if she never got to wear them. She
took the red slip dress from the back of the
closet and found her red leather sandals.

Even after she showered, she was still debating
whether she should wear the dress. Finally, she
put it on. She applied blush and lipstick and
she was ready.

Stuart smiled when she joined him in the
front yard. "I knew it. How could you work at
Lowell's and not have some sexy clothes in re-
serve?"

He took her hand and they walked toward
Main Street. The first restaurant they passed was
a little too crowded, but the second one was just
right. It served a variety of seafood, salads, and
steaks that would allow Stuart to go for something filling and Danita to eat something light.
The restaurant changed the way they were feeling about each other. The medium-sized but
noisy crowd eased some of the tension. They
relaxed. When their order came, Danita was surprised her appetite had returned, but she still
left most of the food on her plate. There was
no need to push her luck healthwise.

After dinner, they walked some more. She
didn't mind that he put his hand on her back
when he steered her around some tricycles, with

small children at the helm and parents following on bikes.

"I love this place," she admitted. She turned to Stuart but saw a flash out of the corner of her eye. She looked around. No one.

They drifted along the street, doing some window-shopping and checking out the menus in the other restaurants. So much of the food sounded good. She didn't object when Stuart selected a chocolate cake layered with strawberry preserves, dark chocolate butter cream and a layer of whipped cream on top.

"You'd better watch it," she warned.

Stuart patted his stomach. "Cast iron."

"Keep it up and we'll see."

"I think we should take another excursion around Sag Harbor."

"We can't. I'm still checking on last-minute details for the store. I want this to be a knock-your-socks-off show."

"Really. You mean I should just return these tickets for *Jekyll and Hyde,* tomorrow night, mezzanine?"

"You're kidding. I really want to see it, and the mezzanine is always best for a short person."

They were standing in front of the house when she whirled around and impulsively kissed him. The kiss deepened until he finally stepped back.

"I—I think this little town makes me crazy. How did you decide on that play?"

"I called the best source I know . . . your mother."

"When did you call her?"

"The night you went to the hospital."

"What? Did you tell her—"

"Calm down. I told her you were asleep and I wanted to surprise you."

She didn't know how to thank him. He was full of surprises. She remembered an article she'd once read, "How to Tell If You're in Love." It contained tips from women who had found love after a long search. One of the women said to get in close quarters, then you'll know if you can stand each other for a lifetime. Without meaning to, she and Stuart had done that. She'd thrown away the adjectives she'd used before to describe him: *ruthless, unprincipled, mercenary,* and replaced them with *strong, fair,* and *very, very sexy.* Why was she having so much trouble admitting she wanted him as much as he wanted her? It wasn't really a question. Danita knew she had fallen in love with Stuart Lowell.

They went inside the house, where they changed into more casual clothes. Stuart chose navy bermuda shorts and a blue and white boatneck sweater, while Danita elected to wear a black capri-length jumpsuit from a new casualwear collection and came down the stairs in her feet bare.

Stuart got a bottle of wine from Tyler's wine cellar and they settled back to watch a movie they both liked, Hitchcock's *Vertigo*. By the middle of the movie, the wine had made them both sleepy, but neither wanted to move. Danita closed her eyes and let her head rest on his shoulder. His first tentative move was to put his arm around Danita and pull her closer. When she didn't resist, he settled back and watched the movie. Unconsciously, he moved his hand to her cheek, then turned and kissed her on the same cheek. She moved her head, and his lips touched hers.

"Nice," she said.

He wasn't sure if she knew what she was doing, and he would not take advantage of her. He liked her kisses, her smooth skin, and the fragrance from her hair. Her skin was flawless even now without makeup. He never liked the layers that his ex-wife wore, but he understood that as an actress she had to be done up. The light from the television was not enough for him to see Danita's face, and he leaned across her to turn on the lamp. Her eyes opened, and he placed a series of kisses on her lips before he slid his tongue into her mouth.

Her arms circled his chest. He knew she was aware of what was happening to him. The kiss deepened until they were breathless. He had never experienced this feeling of desperation. She couldn't lead him this far and stop again.

Danita felt the strong arousal and writhed until she was beneath him. They were fully clothed as they began the dance of love. It was if they were delaying pleasure so it would be more intense.

Each silently told the other what was needed. His hands slid over her body in a tender, possessive manner. Then he sat back. It took her a moment to realize that he had moved away. There was a chill where his warmth had been. She opened her eyes and groaned. "Is that a yes or a no?"

"It's a yes."

She nodded. "Then let's go upstairs." He took her hand and pulled her to her feet. They reached the staircase and he allowed her to go up first. He liked watching her hips swivel. He laughed softly. Somehow, no matter how tiny a black woman was, she had hips that undulated when she walked. It was just a natural fact, he mused. As they reached the top landing, Danita turned and went into her bedroom. He followed. They stretched out side by side, and he leaned over and kissed her again. He caught the top of the zipper of her jumpsuit and gently slid it down to below her waist. She shifted as he pulled the garment from her body, leaving her in skimpy lace panties and bra. His hands slipped inside to the point of her greatest need and teased her until he elicited a sigh.

"Give me a moment," he said, and disappeared down the hall to his room. He returned minutes later with several foil packets of condoms.

He sat on the bed, kicked off his shoes,

pulled his sweater over his head, and in seconds removed his other clothes.

She hadn't waited, but while he was undressing she removed her panties and bra. He rolled over her and was inside with one long thrust. He was both surprised and joyful at the tightness.

She was not a passive lover, as he felt her hands moving along the muscles of his back and around to the abs she had been so impressed with.

Tiny sparks of passion became raging fires of want and turned into smoldering need. Their hips moved in unison until they were exhausted and welcomed the warm release that freed them.

Sometime during the night, they managed to get under the covers. Despite their sated condition, they didn't want to be apart and slept with their arms around each other.

He waited in bed until she woke up the next morning.

"We have to talk."

"I don't have any regrets about last night."

"Neither do I, but if we stay in the same house, it's going to happen again."

"Maybe."

"Definitely."

"Having an affair is going to be tough. We don't know if it's even going to work," she told him.

"I don't think we have a choice."

There was one danger to this affair. There were several board members who would put them through the ringer if they knew. It would be trouble if anyone found out before they wanted it to be public knowledge. They had not decided if this was love or lust.

They had breakfast and made reservations at a midtown hotel. "We'll spend the day in New York. So you can do another complete run-through," Stuart said. "He won't actually perform the magic sequence but we'll get the timing down."

"I'll stop in and pick up another outfit. How do I let you talk me into these things?"

Six

Although Danita gave herself plenty of time to drive to Tyler's office when he summoned her to New York, she was over an hour late because of a traffic accident. Tyler was not a happy camper on that count, and she knew her luck had gone from bad to worse when she saw Hugh Jackson in the office. He was in his late fifties and his hair was silver-gray. He'd had his own firm for a while, but business wasn't good and he'd dissolved his firm and come on board with Lowell's. Danita felt that he resented their success and that may have caused his outburst the one time she'd worked with him.

The office hadn't changed much over the years. Tyler loved his gunmetal gray industrial carpet, black desk, comfortable chair—and secretary. But to Danita the cream-colored walls seemed as cold and sterile as the rest of the office. She wondered how he could work there.

When she was his apprentice, she kept trying to make the office more homey, but he said,

"It's where I work, not where I live. Keep it clean, and that's all that counts."

She'd dressed so carefully for this appointment, she hoped the drive from Sag Harbor hadn't wilted her. She wore a linen dress in fuchsia with a matching rolled-brim hat. Her sandals were a multistriped slingback. As usual, she was a walking advertisement for Lowell's. She'd inherited her style from her mother, who had been reared to believe that a lady always dressed and behaved like a lady.

When Elizabeth had married Darius, Tyler predicted he'd have a son who would one day take over the New York store. When they had only a daughter and then divorced, Tyler said he was skeptical about a female heir. He still needed an heir for the New York store.

Danita's mind kept coming back to Hugh Jackson. Why had Tyler set him up to work with her? If Hugh Jackson thought she was the same little creampuff who'd folded the last time they conflicted, he was sadly mistaken. She had two and a half years more under her belt. She had to fire, hire, reprimand, and reward employees, and she knew how to handle all that now.

For years he'd been the public relations person for the chain of Lowell stores, but Danita's only experience with him was not a good one. It was the second time she had staged an event, and the first was a rousing success. Roses were the theme for this one, and they had every color and species flown in from all over the world to build a float for the special events area. She had left specific instructions with Hugh to watch the float while she went to check on security.

There was a group of high school students visiting D.C., and Hugh decided that it would be a good photo op to have all of the students on the float. While they were setting up the camera, the students started fighting. Before anyone could stop them, they had destroyed the float and done severe property damage.

When Danita returned and confronted Hugh, he lost his temper and started swearing and accusing Danita of deliberately trying to ruin his career. He swore he'd get even with her if he was fired. She didn't care about his threats. She wanted him off the premises.

Tyler had hopped on a shuttle flight and come down to settle the matter. He told Danita about the problems a black PR firm would experience if a black retailer fired him. She gave in, and everything was settled. However, she would not work with Hugh in her store.

"Hugh is handling publicity for the Cancer Society benefit we're having. We were just going over a few things. We can take this up later."

Hugh gave Danita a quick nod and left the room.

"You know, it's time you two patched things up. He's done great work for some of the other stores. Call Skye and ask her."

"I'm sure he's good, but I can't afford some-

one who's going to fly off the handle." She
shuddered as she remembered his six-foot-three
frame standing over her five-foot one and
threatening to make her sorry she ever lived.

"Trust me, he's good."

No one argued about Tyler's business acumen. He'd kept the chain going for sixteen
years. He was a shrewd businessman who could
spot a winning trend, ride it until he'd milked
every possible dime out of it, and let it go before the chain lost money. That was the reason
most of the Godfreys and Lowells apprenticed
under him at the New York store. If Tyler said
they were ready, they got a store to manage.
He'd selected D.C. for Danita because her
mother, who was not a Godfrey by birth, was
managing it only until Danita was ready. While
Elizabeth was the perfect lady and handled any
problem in the store, Danita, under Tyler's tu-
telage, was ready to assume the full responsibil-
ity of running the store.

She and her mother had moved to D.C.
shortly after Danita graduated from high school
and bought a house in the Georgetown section.
Her mother could be sweet, but she was also
strong-willed. While Danita's friends picked colleges like Howard, Elizabeth would let her apply
only to Harvard.

Later, Danita would go to business functions
and see that women who went to predominantly
black colleges had a special alliance with one
another, while her Ivy League background, even

with her magna cum laude status, forced her to
be an outsider.

It also forced her more into the lines that
had been set by three generations before her.
The stores sustained them through hard times,
and the descendants were reaping the rewards
of the good times.

Now the New York store was about to be
passed to another generation. That should have
been Danita, but Stuart had expressed an interest in the position. In fact, as competitive as the
rest of the family members were, Tyler was surprised only Stuart expressed an interest.

Tyler brought Danita out of her trip down
memory lane by mentioning a little problem.
"You've handled special events, and I need your
help. The firm we contracted went belly-up.
Don't ask me why they weren't checked thoroughly. Anyway, I'm stuck, and I need you to
put something together for me."

"Tyler, this is awfully short notice. I don't—"

"Danita, I know you can do this. I also know
that it will be a feather in your cap if you can
pull this off."

She could read between the lines. What he
was actually saying was that if she wanted to get
the board's approval, she would have to do
something spectacular. Stuart had gone out on
a limb with the boutique and had been very
successful. She had to show that she could think
under pressure. She couldn't blow this, or she'd

be stuck in D.C. for the rest of her career with Lowell's.

Tyler's secretary buzzed and announced that Stuart had arrived. Danita's eyes widened as she stared at her uncle. "I invited both of you down, but separately. I couldn't make it look like favoritism. It's too bad you got caught in that delay. We needed some more time to discuss how I can help you."

He shrugged his shoulders and went to get Stuart. Stuart came in. He obviously knew Danita would be there. Knowing that Stuart wanted to make a move to the East Coast and could do it only if he got the New York store or left Lowell's completely brought out Danita's competitive nature.

She didn't want her frustration at having to deal with Hugh Jackson to interfere with her chance at beating Stuart at his own game.

"I guess you want to know why I called you here," Tyler said.

Stuart shook his head. "No. I want to know why you lied about it."

Danita gasped. She hadn't expected anyone to challenge Tyler this way. Stuart walked in and sat down by the desk.

"I didn't exactly lie. I really did need someone to clean up the house a bit. I am thinking of selling it."

"But what's the real reason we're here?" Stuart still pressed for an answer.

"I want to walk you through handling a special benefit for the store."

"We've both done that," Danita said.

"Not in New York and not on the scale that it requires. I'm not saying you aren't good, but I just need to see how much you've learned on your own. Now, I know that Danita does a lot of special event type things, but you haven't."

"I've been too busy trying to get the mud and glass out of the Malibu store."

"Don't get angry. I know you've been working hard. And that was the other reason I wanted you here. I want to talk about Dax."

"What's he done?"

Stuart was two years older than Dax but acted more like a father to him than a brother. The cousins knew it was because their father was a coldhearted man. Alan Lowell could take stripes off you and not break a sweat. While all the children were pushed to succeed, Alan pushed his to such an extent that he could break you rather than help you forward. Stuart had been protected by his mother, but she'd gotten sick and couldn't do the same for Dax. Stuart was away at school and while the cancer ate away at his mother, his father attacked his brother.

After his mother's death, Dax and Stuart learned that she had set up trust funds for them and filtered her wealth into them over the years. The money she had set aside left them comfortable enough so that they could go out on their own. Dax became an international playboy even though he could draw from the trust only at certain times and only in certain amounts.

When he had spent all his money and had to wait for the next check, he came to live with Stuart in California. He enmeshed himself in a decadent lifestyle and told everyone he'd found his home. Stuart would never charge him rent, and Dax drifted only into temporary work. He'd picked up quite a few skills during his travels and always managed to find a job for a few days.

Tyler was now ready to tell them what happened in California. "I spent a week in California, as you know, since Danita challenged me to take on Dax."

"What did you find out?"

"That Dax is intelligent, crafty, and innovative. I think he could take over the California store if you move to New York," he told Stuart.

What was good news for Stuart was bad news for Danita. All of the other stores had successors lined up. New York was the only store that didn't. It was beginning to look as if she would never get out of the nation's capital.

"However, we didn't have one emergency while I was there. So I'm not sure he won't fall apart when we really need him."

"Dammit," Stuart shouted. "You can't treat us like puppets. You lie to us, then promise to tell the truth, and then start rambling. Why don't you just lay it on the line?"

"Okay, okay." Tyler walked behind the desk and sat in the chair. "This is a test for both of you. I don't know which one of you the board will approve. I would like to see you work together, and that's where the packing up the house comes in, and I would like Danita to come up with a little special something that would suit a sophisticated audience."

"Are you serious?" Danita asked. "Are you saying that if we don't get along and we can't put together a program, neither of us will get the New York store?"

"Well, something like that."

"You can't do that."

"Yes, I can. This is a family business. The last one of its kind. We've fought off corporate raiders, ungrateful children, and scandalous behavior. We have every right to decide how we run our business."

"How long is this nonsense going to go on?" Stuart asked.

"About a month. Then I'm going to announce my retirement and turn everything over to one of you."

"You think we can't do it," Danita said. "You don't plan to retire and this is just another carrot being dangled in front of us."

"That's not true."

"I think she's right. How about that Danita and I agree on something. We're going to call your bluff."

"You'll take care of the house and everything?"

"Why not," Danita said. "I'm with Stuart. After all, it's only a month out of our lives."

"Come on, Danita, let's go get something to eat."

"I haven't been to the Olive Garden in some time. Let's go there."

He gave them enough time to get to the elevator, then picked up the phone. "Alan, you know your son. He and Danita are off to bond and show me what they can do."

"We'll push them just enough. I think she'll drop out and you can name Stuart without any problem," Alan replied.

"She has to say she doesn't want the store."

"I know. She's tough in a lot of ways, but I think we're tougher."

Tyler Godfrey and Alan Lowell had been manipulating the lives of every family member connected with Lowell's for sixteen years. Their first move had been to force Darius out in order to get Tyler back in. In a fit of rebellion, Tyler had gone off on his own after college, refusing to kowtow to his parents. They had given the New York store to Darius. When Tyler realized he'd made a mistake, he returned to the fold and worked at the Virginia store with Alan. The two men schemed to get the New York store back and succeeded. Now it was time to scheme again. Alan wanted Stuart to have it and so did Tyler. For all his talk about modern times, he still believed a woman should not have a career.

* * *

Stuart and Danita were at the bar of the Olive Garden having a drink while they waited for their table.

Stuart was on his second drink when the maître d' approached them and led them upstairs and to a table. They perused the menu, and both ordered lasagna.

"Stuart, there is something else going on here. I feel it."

"It's not the first time a predecessor has pulled something like this. Remember what happened with the Georgia store?"

"I'd forgotten. Poor Skye was so torn. She could give up the store and let Aunt Theresa's daughter have it, or she could be a figurehead and let her husband have it. She gets the vote, he runs the store. What a mess."

Of all her cousins, Danita liked Skye the best. At summit meetings they would huddle in a corner, giggling, gossiping, and playing cards. The problem everyone found with Skye was her weight. Her mother was tall and slender and so was her father. Skye did get her parents' height, but she was big-boned and would never be thin. Until she was eighteen she was put on every diet, sent to every fat farm. At one point her mother wanted to hire a hypnotist. But Skye met some big, beautiful women who told her how to be happy with who she was. She'd gained her self-worth but lost the chance to run the store she'd inherited.

"The real problem is that we're all afraid to

walk away. We've been pushed to take command, and when we have a chance, they try to take it away," Stuart said.

"I know, but I really want the store."

"So do I."

"I guess that makes us friendly rivals," Danita said.

"I hope it stays friendly."

After the play they returned to the hotel and the next morning returned to Sag Harbor. They spent the day in individual pursuits. Danita retired early.

Seven

Danita slept late the next morning and enjoyed every minute of it. She'd stayed in bed while she listened for some indication that Stuart was awake. The night before, she'd heard him pacing in his room for hours, and then a couple of times she heard him go downstairs.

About dawn she'd tiptoed down the hall and listened at his door. She could hear his heavy snoring and was glad he'd finally fallen asleep. He'd been pretty angry on the drive back to Sag Harbor. They hadn't talked much but had deliberately avoided mentioning anything that had to do with business. She was falling asleep when they arrived and had begged off a nightcap.

There was danger in what they were doing. She started enjoying the cataloguing and the videos they watched almost every night. The biggest danger for her was that she enjoyed the company. For so many years she'd been content to come home to an empty house, but she didn't think she could ever do that again. She'd have to get a cat.

She heard the doorbell and ignored the first three rings. Then, thinking it might be an emergency, she jumped out of bed and grabbed an oversized T-shirt. Barefoot, she ran down to the door and peered through the one-way window. Tyler had installed it when she lived there so she could see the person on the outside clearly and didn't need a peephole.

It was Hugh Jackson. She took a deep breath and opened the door.

"Good morning, Ms. Godfrey."

"Good morning. What are you doing here?"

"Mr. Godfrey wanted you to have this. It's some PR I did for some of the other stores. He also wants you to have this." He gave her a sealed envelope.

It wasn't the first time Tyler had something delivered to her. It was just the timing. They'd seen him only a few hours earlier, and they would see him the next day. Why was this so important? Unless what Jackson was really doing for Tyler was spying on them.

"He had you deliver this rather than mail it?"

"He forgot to give it to you and this was the best way."

"Thank you very much for your trouble."

She was just about to close the door, when Stuart came downstairs wearing nothing but low-slung jeans and a bleary-eyed look.

"Hello, Mr. Lowell." Although Jackson didn't

change his facial expression, his voice deepened. He saluted and walked away.

Stuart moved closer to Danita and said, "What was that all about?"

"I don't know, but I think you just provided fuel for the fire."

"Sorry. I wasn't expecting company."

"Well, he'll go back and say we looked as if we're getting along."

She went outside to see if Hugh was still around, and she could see his car as it disappeared down the driveway.

"He said that he wanted us to have this."

Danita looked over the items that involved PR and Stuart looked over the data on the security people. Then they exchanged papers and talked about their choices. Danita had four items that she liked, but nothing struck her as what she wanted for the benefit.

The security was another matter. She looked at the kind of training they'd had. He looked at the places they'd worked.

"Why does that make a difference?"

"It means experience. This group can mobilize quickly."

"I don't think we need that after all. It's in a store, not on top of a mountain. If we give the other team the job, then they'll be getting experience."

They argued back and forth until she finally had Stuart choose. He selected the Mario Kingston Company.

Once that was done, they called Tyler. He was surprised by the security choice but didn't have any qualms about hiring them on such short notice rather than using store security.

For the first time since they'd been in Sag Harbor, Danita went for a swim. After a few laps, she saw Stuart come out of the house, but he didn't have on a swim suit. He stood and watched her. Finally, she stopped swimming and pulled up to the shallow end. "Why are you just standing there, gawking at me?"

"I'm not gawking. I'm admiring your form."

"Yeah, right!"

"You are a very good swimmer. But you know that."

"It's the one exercise I like." She had discovered swimming by accident. All the kids learned to swim but none had liked it too much, especially the girls. They spent hours pulling together a look and they weren't going to mess up their hair by jumping in a pool. Skye's mother had read that swimming was good for losing weight and packed her off to an instructor. Danita went along for the ride. She had so much fun that she kept going even after Skye gained ten pounds and her mother gave up on the swimming idea.

"You don't have to exercise much."

She laughed. She probably exercised more than people who had weight problems. She exercised to build muscle. She had seen what the aging process did. As much as people talked about being thin, it was the heavier people who looked healthier when they got older. Thin people seemed to go to skin and bone.

After a few more laps, she climbed out of the pool. Stuart held out a towel for her.

"Do you think he'll say we're sleeping together?" she asked.

"Probably."

"That doesn't bother you." It was a statement, not a question.

"No, it doesn't. It's true, and one day we won't be able to hide it. Just because there are two rooms with lights on at night doesn't mean that the people around here don't think we're sleeping together. They just can't be sure, and as long as we keep it that way, we'll be fine."

She was beginning to like him more and more. He had qualities she'd never thought of connecting to Stuart Lowell. But how would the family feel?

"We have let our family dictate our work life; let's not let them dictate our home life."

It was time to find another movie. Tonight they chose a romantic comedy. The hero and heroine lived in the same apartment and didn't know each other, but agreed to the arrangement. He worked nights, she worked days, and they would just leave each other notes. "You forgot to put the toilet seat down." "Here's my half of the rent." Then he got sick and they finally met and fell in love.

"There is no way I could do that," she said. "Live in a house with someone I never saw. It would make me crazy."

"I think it might be fun. Come on, think about us," Stuart said. "We are so close on some things and so far apart on others."

"Yes, like movies. You like suspense and I like comedy."

"Food—I prefer really spicy stuff and you like mild."

"Books."

"Yeah, not the ones on the library shelf. The ones by your bed that are battered from rereading.

"Come to Malibu," Stuart added quickly.

She didn't say anything.

"I'm serious. Come see how I live. I want you to know all about me."

"Then you can come to D.C."

They had known each other all their lives and had never extended that invitation. The home was the last fortress against the world, and they were both very careful about who they let get that close.

"If . . . when I come to Malibu," Danita continued, "am I going to see your life or your brother's?"

"Definitely mine. I refuse to allow my brother to touch anything of mine. He'll mix it with his and then pretend he doesn't know what I'm talking about when I claim my things. He has the guest house and I have the main house."

"You're very close."

"We had to be. Dad can be—he wants it his way or not at all. Dax needs to find his own way."

"Tyler thinks he's going to take over for you."

"Tyler is wrong. Dax knows how to pretend, but once everything's settled here, Dax will do what's best for him."

"You two decided that before you came here."

"You are a very smart lady."

Stuart was surprised that she picked up on what the brothers had arranged. His brother hated corporate life with a passion. There was no way he would take over one store in California, much less two, and Stuart didn't want him to do it.

He shouldn't have been surprised by Danita's observation. She had been picking up on all the little clues, but she still said something else was happening. He hadn't told her, but there was no way he would let her go. He would find a way for both of them to be in New York even if he had to leave the family business. They would be together. He just needed to find the right time to tell her.

Only after she had returned to her room did she remember that the old adage was true. "Living well is the best revenge." That's how she, Stuart, and Dax could foil all of them. As soon as this benefit was over, they would sit down and make some decisions about where they were going.

Family grapevines would always exist. Little seeds of doubt had been planted, expanded and soon everyone thought they knew secrets that the outside world would never suspect. How many times had she heard gossip about Stuart's marital problems. Most of the talk said it was his fault. Even Skye had once said that Stuart might be more like his father. Alan never seemed to show emotion.

Danita had believed Stuart was ruthless and cold-hearted until her illness. She'd seen the tender, caring side of Stuart and she knew that he would never be like Alan.

When they were having dinner that night, she told him about her thoughts. He laughed and said she didn't want to know what was being said about her. She convinced him that she did want to know.

"Well, for one, they think you are very . . . smart."

"You rat. I thought you were going to tell me some gossip."

"That's what they think. They also think that you're reaching too high for the man in your life. The cousins say you want too much, and since you'll never get it, you're going to be an old maid."

"Do you think I want too much?" All she could think about was that earlier that day she was thinking of getting a cat. Now it really sounded like something an old maid would do.

"I don't know what you want, except for that fantasy you told me about."

"I want someone who won't be afraid of my brain."

"I know what you mean. Remember my friend Sam Winston?"

"That was a hunk." She remembered the tall, dark college sophomore who moved with the grace of a cat. Stuart brought him to the opening of the Florida store. All the girls were trying to sit next to him, get his attention. He broke all their hearts by dating his neighbor's daughter.

"Well, he liked you. He thought you were a Kewpie doll and he asked me if he could ask you out. You were seventeen. You had on this blue dress that fit like a glove. Well, anyway, I told him to ask you to go to the movies. He walked over to where you and the cousins were standing, and you were explaining the difference between stocks, bonds, and mutual funds. The brother couldn't handle the fact that you knew all those things."

She paused for a second. "So being smart is a handicap."

"No. I could never understand why he walked away. If I hadn't already had a date, I would have jumped at the chance to go out with you. I liked the fact that you were smart.

"Do you want to get married?" he asked.

"Yes . . . I think so."

"Then don't settle. That will make you miserable."

He didn't say it, but she knew he was talking about Nikki.

They both sat quietly for a minute. Then Stuart said, "Don't ever be anything other than what you are. Let the man who's right for you find you. If you try to change, he won't recognize you."

She was torn. On the one hand, she found Stuart charming and sexy and she liked being with him, but now she found he was even more. He was a friend, a lover, but she couldn't allow herself to go further. He had to be the one to say he was ready to make a commitment. After his divorce he didn't seem to want another relationship. He'd dated, but he'd never made another commitment.

"Tell me something you do that no one else knows," she said to Stuart.

"Only if you'll return the favor."

She nodded. "What is it?"

"I write poetry. Not very good poetry, but it's fun for me."

"How do you know it's not very good?"

"I sent it to a magazine and got rejected."

"How many times?"

"Once was enough."

She shook her head. "You can't let one person tell you it's not good." She couldn't imagine Stuart letting anyone tell him what he could or couldn't do. That was one of his strengths. Rejections became challenges, and he was always able to prove people wrong.

"What do you want me to do? Keep sending in my poems until I can do what that guy did a few years ago—use the rejection letters for wallpaper? I think not."

"How about sending them in until one gets published?"

"Never mind. What's your secret?"

"I don't have any."

"You little cheat." He grabbed her and started tickling her. "Come on, tell me!"

They rolled on the floor, laughing, until she finally yelled, "I'll tell you."

She sat up and looked him in the eye. "I collect salt and pepper shakers. I have hundreds of them. Even my mother doesn't tell anyone I do that. She thinks it's strange that someone who doesn't do a lot of cooking collects them."

They stayed on the floor until she felt Stuart slip his hand under her and pull her toward him. She allowed him to do this until they were face-to-face. His eyes were filled with passion, but there was something else there too. Tenderness. She leaned forward and kissed him, first lightly, then with everything in her. She didn't need him to make the commitment. She had made hers. She wanted this man, and if she couldn't have him forever, she would be happy with this time.

That night she lay in bed but she wasn't

sleepy. It was an unwritten law that they did not sleep in the same bed. Stuart was the one who always went back to his own room. He kept the light on a timer so it would go off and on. He wanted anyone outside to know that they slept in separate rooms. She didn't care anymore, but it was important to him. She knew that if Tyler was going to sell the house, she was going to buy it. She and Stuart were making too many memories for her to let someone else have it.

Eight

Things moved quickly after Danita and her crew sat down and discussed her game plan. She'd talked to store department heads and borrowed a valued employee from each section. Once they realized that she was open to suggestion and quite fair with giving credit, they came up with more ideas about seating, coat closets, and anything that would help make the benefit a success.

Danita's mother called to wish her well.

"I'm proud of you, baby. I hope they take a lot of pictures so I can have some souvenirs of your big night. Oh, by the way, Alan called. He said that he needs to talk to Tyler right away but can't get him."

"We recruited his secretary, so unless Tyler's in the office, the machine will pick up. I'll give him the message."

Stuart came by for moral support more than anything else. He kept telling Danita she was terrific and had a natural talent for organization.

"You do what you have to do" is all she said.

* * *

He arrived one afternoon and saw a group of her recruits, probably in their late teens, taking a smoking break. His first thought was to lecture them about the habit, but he could see that they were very animated about something.

He walked by them and heard them talking about Danita.

"Can you believe it?" one of them said. "I just went up to her and made a suggestion and she said I was right on target."

"I know. Girl, can you imagine working for her all the time?"

"I bet you'd never call in sick."

"You can't. When you're working on something like this, you need to be here every day. She always looks great. I'm going to ask her how she does it. I wish the payroll section were open before Friday. I'd get something really special to wear to the benefit."

"I'm checking out this event-planner course at one of the colleges. All that and a fine man like Stuart Lowell."

"You think a little somethin' somethin' is going on?"

"It would be if I were her."

"Have you checked out that security chief Mario . . ."

He didn't stay around to hear the rest of the conversation, but it was obvious Danita had made a difference in how these young women thought. It reminded him of his relationship with his California staff. Even though he was the boss and they knew it, they trusted him. It was also obvious he and Danita were not as discreet as they thought they were being.

Stuart looked around for Mario Kingston and found the security chief checking all the big-screen monitors. They had never had an event take place in the store before this one.

"How's it going?"

"We have everything under control. The store will be closed down tomorrow night, my men will do a hard-target search to make sure no one is hiding in any of the nooks and crannies, and we'll just stay alert."

Stuart nodded and left the man to do the job. He felt completely confident in Mario and his team.

He went inside and found Danita with members of the committee from the Cancer Society. Everything had to be timed so that the speeches were over by nine-thirty P.M. and the show was over by eleven.

Lowell's NY had Pardon Our Appearance signs all over the fifth floor. The stage was being set for the biggest extravaganza of the year. The press had interviewed Danita about the differences in production between D.C. and New York. They had only two more days until show time.

The invitations had been sent out even before Danita arrived, and people had responded quickly. They were prepared if some who did not respond arrived anyway.

Danita was walking through the act with Jeff, the magician, while she checked the seating arrangement. Hugh Jackson was milling around, and she recruited him.

"Didn't you handle things in D.C.?" she asked. "We could use some help."

"Yes, this was a good project to work on. I always said if I had the chance, I'd like to be part of it."

"Well, now you are. Jeff will tell you what he needs."

He seemed much more nervous than she had ever seen him as he followed Jeff around the scenery.

Stuart had just arrived. "Was that Hugh? What's he doing here?"

"I think he came to see Wendy, so I gave him an assignment backstage with Jeff."

"He's seeing Wendy?"

"Can you believe that? I've seen them around the store all week. I like older couples."

"Me too, except when they seem to be getting together more than we are."

"What can we do about that?"

"Sneak off to my hotel room or yours? Isn't that why we have long-term stays? So that we can go to the hotel anytime."

"We'll see. I have to find Tyler. Your father wants to speak to him."

"He's with Mario. If I see him first, I'll tell

him to call. Special Events has a hundred things
going on at one time, and you don't even seem
frazzled."

"I love doing this. I could do it day and
night. There's Tyler. I'll give him an update.
Project planning is the best."

He didn't know how hard it was to put one
of these benefits on. He'd done one fashion
show when he opened the boutique and felt
ready for a body bag. He'd turned the rest of
the programs over to Laura and hadn't done
any since she'd left almost six months before.
Danita handled everything quickly and effi-
ciently.

He might think of hiring someone if he went
back to the California store. For the first time
since he'd arrived in New York, he wasn't so
sure he would get Tyler's seat. It was time for
him to drop the macho act and admit to her
that if she won, he would be there to support
her.

Before she reached Tyler, one of the young
women Stuart had overheard earlier came up to
Danita.

"Ms. Godfrey, could I bother you for just a
moment?"

"Of course, Cathryn." Danita looked at Stuart, and he realized it was going to be one of
those girl-talk things.

Cathryn had been one of the last people selected for the project and one of the hardest
workers. Danita had been skeptical since she'd

been absent quite a bit. But once they got started, the young woman was like a sponge. She soaked up her brief training and applied it. Danita was thinking of pulling her out of the pack and making her an administrative assistant.

"I'll be with Tyler," he said, and kept walking.

Danita and Cathryn found a quiet area and sat down. "What's on your mind?"

"I . . . we really enjoyed working with you and I'm thinking of becoming an event planner. But anyway, this is the problem. We normally get paid on Friday, and the benefit is on Thursday, so we won't be able to buy anything new to wear to it. And we want to look nice. . . ."

"First I'm going to give you some hard facts. You must learn to manage your money. Go to seminars, buy books, and read them thoroughly."

Cathryn nodded. "I understand." She turned to leave, but Danita caught her hand.

"I gave you the hard facts first because I want you to listen to me." She pulled out her cell phone and punched in a few numbers. "Agnes, it's Danita Godfrey. The morning of the benefit, I'm sending the six young women who will be representing the store over to you. I want you to do a complete makeover and find something in the designers' section for them to wear. Whatever you find is theirs to keep."

"Ms. Godfrey, the girls are going to die when I tell them. Thank you so much."

"Don't do that. Let it be a surprise," Danita told her.

"Yes, Ma'am. I can keep a secret."

Cathryn scampered off and Danita joined Tyler and Stuart in Tyler's office. His secretary had been recruited to help with some other parts of the show. The two things Danita had learned in D.C. were that if the staff was involved, they felt like part of the program and they enjoyed a break in what could sometimes be a monotonous day. Give them something to remember the day and you have loyal employees.

"You've done a fabulous job, Danita," Tyler said.

"Thank you."

"Special Events has so many pieces to the puzzle, I'd be a basket case."

"Tyler Godfrey," a voice said. "Where have you been?"

Two pairs of eyes turned to match the face to the voice. The only one who didn't turn around was Tyler.

The woman swept into the office. "I'm Claudine Hamilton." She was about sixty, and her mink was draped over one shoulder, revealing an asymmetrically buttoned white suit with gold trim and a slim white skirt.

"I'm Danita Godfrey."

"I'm Stuart Lowell."

"I've heard so much about you. It's nice to meet you at last."

"What do you want, Claudine?" Tyler asked gruffly.

"A teeny, teeny favor. I need another ticket to the show."

"I don't know—"

Stuart interrupted. "I'm sure we can find something for your friend, Tyler." He opened the desk drawer, pulled out a batch of tickets, peeled one off, and gave it to Claudine.

"Thank you, darling man." She walked over to Tyler and kissed him on the cheek. "I'm having a little get-together after the function. Would you be able to come?"

"Thanks, but I—I'm on another project."

"Nice meeting you," she said to Stuart and Danita, and glided out of the room as easily as she had come in.

"Come on, Uncle Tyler. Tell your favorite niece what's going on. Oh, I almost forgot, Alan wants you to call him."

"Looks like a wedding to me," said Stuart.

"Don't get started. That woman is always following me around and asking for favors."

"Is that all?" Danita asked teasingly.

"No, that's not all. She's been dropping hints about marriage."

"Now, have you been leading her on, Tyler?" Stuart joined Danita in teasing him.

The glare said it all. Tyler was not talking about the woman.

"I've got to make a phone call," Tyler said as he left his office.

"I think Tyler's got a girlfriend."

"I think he doesn't want a girlfriend."

"I told you, I like to see older couples. It makes me think it might happen to me. It could happen to you. You are a hopeless romantic.

"The plans are really coming together."

"Are you finished for the day?"

She nodded. He waited for Danita while she made sure everything that needed to be done was being handled by her staff. Then she met Stuart outside the store.

Tyler dialed Alan's number knowing he had more bad news than good news for him. "She's handling herself just fine. She's got all the young girls wanting to be like her and all the men wanting to date her."

"Then Darius will win. We can't have that, Ty. You've got to do something to make this a job she doesn't want."

"I'm trying. It's just not working. Her father has us by the short hairs, and he doesn't even know what's going on."

"Well, that's what comes of making a deal with the devil."

"We have to remember he was threatening to tear us down, Alan. We didn't have any other choice. So let me deal with what's happening. I'll call you when I've got something to tell you."

By the time he got off the phone with Alan,

Tyler needed a drink. He left the store and went across the street into a little restaurant. He'd just ordered his favorite martini, when a soft voice called to him. Claudine. His day was getting worse.

Although his hotel was only a few blocks from the store, Stuart hailed a taxi. If it had been rush hour, they probably would have walked.

After looking around to make sure there was no one in the hall, Stuart leaned down and kissed her as he put his card key in the lock. As soon as he closed the door to his room, they began undressing. Never had he felt the need to be with a woman, to be in her, as he did with this one. He hadn't sneaked off to a hotel since he was seventeen. He couldn't imagine staying at different hotels but Danita insisted. She said it would avoid distractions.

He tried to rationalize his feelings, since they had been unable to spend nights together while she worked on this benefit. Even as he had the thought, he knew it was a lie. He'd gone for months without sex from the time he'd separated from his wife, through the divorce, and only when he spent time with Danita had it become a problem. Control was his strong point, except with her. All she had to do was look at him and smile and he was lost. Perhaps that was the reason they fought so much. They knew that if they weren't angry with each other, another feeling would take over, and neither wanted that to happen.

Sometime during the night, they managed to get under the covers. Despite their sated condition, they didn't want to be apart and slept with their arms around each other.

He waited until she woke up.

"We have to talk."

"I don't have any regrets about last night."

"Neither do I, but we can't do this again until we get home."

"Maybe."

"Definitely."

There was one danger to this affair. There were several board members who would not approve if they knew. It would be trouble if anyone found out before they wanted it public knowledge. They had not decided if this was love or lust.

Danita opened the door to retrieve the complimentary newspaper the hotel left outside each room. She had made a cup of coffee from the set up the hotel provided and wanted to peruse the paper while Stuart was getting dressed.

The headlines blared something about the President's European trip, but at the bottom of a column was the teaser "Is there finally going to be a union between the Lowells and Godfreys? See page 4." She opened the paper and shivered. There were pictures of Stuart carrying her into the house in Sag Harbor the night he brought her home from the hospital. Of course, it didn't look like she was sick in the picture. There were pictures of them sitting by the pool, and the most damaging was a large picture of her kissing Stuart at the door to their hotel room.

Stuart was whistling as he came out of the bathroom, ready for the day. He looked at Danita and knew that something was wrong. He was hoping she wouldn't be filled with regrets about the night before. As he approached, he saw the paper and the pictures and swore softly but distinctly.

"I can't believe we didn't know we were being followed."

Stuart slammed his fist against the desk. "How could I have been so stupid? I've always protected the women in my life. And the one time I let my guard down, this is what happens."

"Don't beat up on yourself too much. I certainly knew what I was doing."

Given the time they had spent together and the pleasure they'd gained, Danita could not believe she had been so careless. She still wasn't sure how she felt about him. Was it love? Was it passion? He'd never said the words to her, and no matter what anyone said, the words were important. She never imagined she and Stuart could get along, much less become lovers.

Her face grew hot as she thought of the things they did and the possibility there was someone with a telescopic lens watching them. It was the ultimate violation, and she would have to live with it.

She needed to return to familiar territory and regroup. This was something that Stuart would not like but might be necessary in order for her to make some sense of what had happened. From the time that stringer recognized her, she should have known someone had taken interest in her, but why?

"I guess the only way to get through this is to ignore it."

"You're kidding!"

The media storm that greeted them was one reserved for major politicians and movie stars. The security was just as tough. They set up barricades as they directed the taxi to pull up to the side entrance and help Stuart and Danita inside.

As the two were escorted through the gauntlet, Danita could hear her name being called by people waving notebooks and cameras.

"This is ridiculous," she said. "It shouldn't be happening to us. We aren't celebrities." They had made it to Tyler's office.

"I'm afraid you are now," Mario Kingston told her. "Don't worry. I've seen this kind of thing before. There'll be a new story in a couple of weeks and you'll be forgotten."

"I can't wait a couple of weeks. I have a benefit tomorrow night."

"Ms. Godfrey, please understand. You cannot control this. I will guarantee you the protection from this group," he said. "Now, here's the way we work. I'll draw up the plans and we'll discuss modifications."

"What about the customers?" Stuart asked.

"No, sir, as soon as the paper hit the stands this morning, I saw what was happening and contacted Tyler Godfrey. He gave me the authority to do what I felt was best. I closed the store and allowed only staff with identification in."

"You did a great job." Stuart was impressed.

"That's what I'm paid for."

Mario was gone before Danita could thank him. Now that she felt safe, she remembered all the things she had to do.

"I'm going to use the conference room and get this all together. Then it might be the best thing if I left."

"Why?"

"I want the reporters here for the benefit, not because they're interested in my love life."

"I'm going to talk to Jackson. That is, if Mario let him in."

He and Danita laughed at the fear the no-nonsense man could generate. "Thanks for selecting him, Stuart. I don't think the other firm could have done it."

"It's like I told you, experience over friend-ship."

As she started for the conference room, she heard Tyler in the hall, swearing a blue streak. He stopped only when he saw Danita and Stuart.

"This man thinks I can't find my own office by myself."

"I'm so sorry, Uncle Tyler," Danita began.

"I warned you to be careful. Now we just have to wait until the dust settles. I may have to stay on the board another couple of months."

"Do you think this will be over by then?"

"We'll find a way. Is that PR person around?"

"Stuart went to get him."

Danita felt the pain begin right under her breastbone. She fumbled in her handbag, found her antacids, and took two of them.

She looked up to find Tyler staring at her. "It's nothing big. I ate something that didn't agree with me, and it still feels like it's in my system."

Stuart returned with Jackson, who made a few calls and said his contact told him that the pic-tures were dropped off by a messenger to all the papers. Only this paper thought it was news and printed the pictures. Somehow word of mouth made them important.

"Now the other papers want something," Stu-art said. "I'm going to track down the person who took those pictures, and believe me, he will be very sorry."

"Before you run through this fire in a gasoline suit, think it through. We don't need a picture of you beating someone up about a picture of me."

He put is arm around Danita. "I don't know, maybe we could sell the story."

Danita began laughing and couldn't stop.

"It wasn't that funny."

"It's just the idea that yesterday the people outside that door didn't know who I was, and today they think we're on a first-name basis."

"That's what happens when there's a slow day as far as the newspapers are concerned."

"Where do we go from here?"

Hugh Jackson had handled publicity for the chain for six years and advised them to treat it as lovers discovered. They must never treat it as a fling, but a serious romance, even if they broke up in a couple of weeks.

"I'm going down to talk to them. We may have to hold a press conference and be very cautious about what we say."

He returned twenty minutes later with the arrangement. "They are going to work through my office. I reminded them that the benefit was the most important thing, and we would add a section for the press, but no interviews until after the benefit."

"And they bought it?" Tyler asked.

"For now."

Stuart said he would make arrangements for a press seating. After Jackson left, he turned to the others. "Something isn't right with this. I'm going to ask Mario to make sure that only the people his men know have access to the backstage area."

"You think the press wants something else?" Danita asked.

"Yes. I don't think those pictures should have brought that crowd. Every one of us should be on the lookout for strangers, or even employees out of place."

Nine

The fifth floor of Lowell's was their special event area. They held everything from plays to fashion shows to benefits such as the one they were having tonight. It was another reason Danita wanted the New York store. None of the other stores had areas with this much space. New York was so different, with all the programs held there and all the nonprofit agencies that needed a place for fund-raisers.

The Cancer Society benefit, now taking on the atmosphere of a movie premiere, was in full swing as long rows of limousines formed outside the store. The chauffeurs pulled up to the front door and the beautiful people stepped out, waving to the crowd. Then the cars pulled away quickly. Media darlings stepped to the microphones for quick interviews, giving reasons for their support of the Cancer Society, expounding on what they hoped to accomplish, and, of course, showing off the designer gowns they wore.

To her surprise, Danita noticed Tyler's chauffeur. *I guess he has a better handle on how to travel around the city now,* she thought. She made her way through the crowd, accepting compliments, comparing notes, and checking with security for anything suspicious.

Danita struck up a conversation with an actor from a new sitcom that debuted to gigantic ratings. His success story was the envy of every actor. A year ago he was telling jokes in bars for very little money, and now his per-episode salary was about to move from five figures to six.

"Congratulations on your show," she said.

"Congratulations on yours," he said as he looked at the huge crowd. "I'd like to know how you managed to pull all of this together."

"I did something like this for our store in D.C.," she began.

"Maybe we could have lunch and talk about it?"

"Maybe she's too busy for lunch."

Danita and the actor turned to find a stone-faced Stuart Lowell glaring at them. The actor beat a hasty retreat.

"You didn't have to do that," Danita said.

"Too many of these kids get money before they know what to do with it."

"They need a week with Tyler."

"They also think it means they can get any woman they want." She didn't want to have that conversation, so she started walking to the reception line. Stuart followed, since he was part of it.

Stuart and Danita were on the reception line as the mayor, senators, and assorted politicians joined the charity leaders and contributors for news photos. The men wore designer tuxedos and most of the women wore long gowns, many of them purchased at Lowell's.

Danita knew she would be moving through the crowd and backstage, so she'd opted for a short white eyelet dress with a fully lined skirt and a scalloped edge. Her short hair was pulled back and held with golden combs. Her strappy gold sandals completed her outfit. It was from a new American designer whom she'd discovered on a trip to the Bahamas.

Inside, there was a frenzy of activity as the workers completed the set minutes before the curtain went up. People were still dashing around, checking makeup, costumes, and, especially, props. Although he was working PR for the Lowell's chain, Hugh Jackson had been enlisted to move props, and Danita noticed him scurrying around with the others. They hadn't seen each other since Danita had accepted Tyler's project, for which Danita was grateful. Jackson was convinced Danita tried to get him fired for using abusive language when she reprimanded him for misplacing a key. But that was not at all the case.

In spite of all the activity occupying Danita's mind, she could not stop thinking about the Sag Harbor house. She really wanted it. Even if she stayed with the D.C. store, she could use it for getaways.

They had invited Stuart's father to the benefit. Danita had wanted to show a strong supportive family and since she was now involved with Stuart, it seemed natural to invite Alan. But he refused. Danita wondered if he was becoming more reclusive. She made a mental note to mention it to Stuart and then made her way to her seat.

Danita sat in the mezzanine, commonly regarded as the owner's section, waiting for Stuart and Tyler to join her. Danita preferred to sit in that area because she could see better from higher up.

Stuart soon arrived and whispered that Tyler was engrossed in a conversation with some business cronies and wouldn't be joining them.

"We have to meet with a couple of board members when this is over."

The speakers finished and the show began. It was a combination ballet and magic show.

The theme of the show was that a woman had been kidnapped. Her lover, the magician, scales the walls of the medieval castle she is being held in and is captured. For the rest of the show the magician performs tricks to enable him to rescue his lady love from a large brown safe. The prop safe was always brown. The skit had been written especially for a D.C. performance and translated successfully to the New York facility.

She'd love to have this larger space to put on other, more ambitious events.

The kidnapper put the woman into the safe and planned to force the magician to watch her die. The large safe was suspended over the audience. Finally, with all that he could summon, the lover cast a spell on the safe. It broke open and instead of the woman falling out, Monopoly money covered the people below. The woman then appeared in the audience in another outfit.

As they watched the play, something nagged in the back of Danita's mind. Something was wrong. The prop safe was not brown but gray! As soon as the show was over, she had to go to her temporary office to check. She'd selected an office in the store that wasn't being used.

The back of the store had winding staircases, near the freight elevators, that employees used but were not open to the public. It was sometimes easier to transport clothes and supplies on the staircases rather than in the sections used by the customers.

The second safe was in an office in this section. It usually held the employees payroll but tonight it had been moved from the cashier's cage to this office. Mario had insisted on taking it out of the store and putting it into a less accessible office. Danita was amazed at how many people preferred to give cash instead of a check. Although canceled checks were proof of charitable donations, cash seemed to be given from the heart.

Hugh Jackson was standing near the back of the room, and she walked over to him. "You were in D.C. Are you sure there's no danger to the audience with that safe?"

"Yes, ma'am. I saw this trick a couple of times. The audience goes wild."

"You've been practicing with them?"

"Just a little. I brought the safe in the side door."

Stuart joined her at the foot of the staircase. "The last of the donations are in. I'll have Wendy take them up to the office safe, and security will pick them up in about fifteen minutes."

"Okay. I'll see you later. I'm going to my office to check on the second safe." She turned and walked to the elevator.

Because of the noisy throng, Stuart had heard only part of what she said, something about a safe. He'd find out what she'd said later, when they joined Tyler and the other board members. He didn't think this was a friendly meeting. The publicity about a possible affair wasn't a problem with most of the people who read about it, but it could become one in the boardroom. He recalled a few years before how the board had passed over the eldest brother at Lowell's OH when it was discovered he had fathered an illegitimate child. That was part of the problem with a family-owned company. Their rules were handed down from the previous generation, and the family could cut you off at whim.

When Stuart arrived on the employees-only level, he looked for Wendy. She would have the donation checks and any cash that was contributed. This would be given to the security men.

He couldn't find her. He used his master pass and opened the cashier's cage. There was a space where another safe should be.

Danita waved to the guard as she entered her temporary office. She went straight to the desk and turned on the lamp, and then the computer. As she fumbled through the file cabinet, she heard a noise. She turned and came face-to-face with Hugh Jackson.

"What are you doing here?"

"You've ruined everything."

"What are you talking about, Hugh?"

The man came out of the darkness, and she saw he had a gun. "Don't scream." He backed up and turned on the overhead fluorescent lights. Danita saw a crate on skids. In the crate was the safe, the brown one that should have been used in the play. Her eyes widened and she turned back to Jackson.

"What's going on?"

"You just got yourself in more trouble, missy. All you had to do was stay downstairs for ten more minutes. Just ten. I'd be gone and no one would be the wiser."

"You told them to bring that safe. But that's the one from the cashier's cage. It's the one with the money." She knew that later that night there would be additional checks, so what could he want? Then it dawned on her. The payroll was in the safe. They had made an arrangement with the bank. Lowell's employees could cash their check on the premises, and the money was in the safe. That's why the safe had been changed. The store's safe was brown. The gray one was an extra safe that someone brought in.

Someone opened the door. Danita turned to Wendy, who had been downstairs, collecting donations. "Get help!" she cried.

The older woman came in and closed the door. Now Danita realized she was part of this elaborate scheme. She'd been accepting the donations and locking them in the safe in the cashiers cage all week.

"We're going to get caught," Wendy whined. "I never should have let you talk me into this. I'm too old to go to prison."

"Shut up. We can pull this off," Jackson assured his accomplice.

"What should I do?" Wendy asked.

"We have to make an adjustment. Go bring the car around to the back. I'll bring the safe down the freight elevator."

Wendy nodded and left.

"Can't believe it, can you? Two old people have outsmarted you."

"This isn't going to work."

"Oh, yes, it will. The guards are so used to me pushing a safe around that they won't care about me until it's over. It would be over now if you hadn't come in."

There was a knock on the door. Jackson waved the gun, and Danita knew it was an order to keep quiet.

"What do you want?" he called out.

"It's time for the pickup."

Jackson moved close to Danita. "Tell him it's downstairs with Lowell," he whispered. She did as she was told.

"Thank you, ma'am. Sorry to have disturbed you."

The departing footfalls made Danita's heart pound. Her last chance at rescue was fading into the distance. Jackson couldn't let her live. *Think. Think,* she told herself. Then she realized he couldn't shoot her. The guards were too close. He didn't have a chance to lock the door. All she had to do was get to the desk and press the alarm.

He stepped away to check the safe. He was a big man and would have no trouble moving it to the freight elevator. He'd practiced too many times. He just had to take care of her.

Danita ran to the desk, but she couldn't get behind it to press the alarm. Jackson grabbed her and tossed her against the window. She fell. He picked up a paperweight from the desk.

Jackson had her cornered. "You know what it's like to be a man and have some little snip of a girl give you orders?"

Danita pulled herself to her feet, backed up,

and tried to edge her way around the room. "I don't understand."

"You wouldn't. I hate this job. All you fat cats. You know how many people get old and never have enough money to live on? Health insurance alone takes most of your money."

"What about investments?" she asked, trying to stall Jackson.

"Not everyone invests, saves. Some of us live paycheck to paycheck."

Danita wanted to say it wasn't her fault if he didn't manage his money, but she knew that would only make him angrier.

"Throwing your weight around because you can. You tried to have me fired over a little mistake. That's when I knew I'd find a way to get you."

The man was insane. He was blaming Danita for his failures and he had involved a trusted employee with his scheme. She knew there was no way to talk to him. The best thing she could do was try to get to the door. Before she could move, Jackson caught her sleeve and threw her to the floor again.

Danita didn't remember screaming. She just saw Jackson's raised hand clutching the paperweight and then he was jerked back. She scrambled to her feet and saw Stuart struggling with the man. They fell on the floor and rolled by the desk. Stuart pulled his arm back and Danita heard a sharp crack. Jackson's eyes rolled back in his head, and he wobbled as he stepped forward and fell, facefirst to the floor.

"What a fight," Tyler said from the doorway.

She had never seen Stuart fight. She couldn't even remember anyone telling her he'd had a fight.

Security and the police came in and dragged the still-unconscious man out.

"What were you thinking, coming in here late at night?" Stuart asked.

"I remembered something about the project with the roses I did in D.C. There was a full record of my exact instructions on disk. Jackson said he never got those instructions, but later he mentioned the side door. It led to the driveway for deliveries. I had a truck waiting to take the roses to hospitals and clinics. Since he said he never got the instructions, the roses were taken through the front door and around to the truck."

"What about the door?"

"I gave him a key to that door. He told me he lost it. Then he brought it to me the next day. I thought he just forgot he had it."

"He had someone make a copy? Why go through all that trouble?"

"To get to that." Danita pointed to the safe that was still on the skid, ready to be taken out.

"He was just a common thief?"

"Not so common. He breached security, not by sneaking in but by walking boldly down the hall and into this office. He's moved large objects from one place to another, and who would think he had the safe with the payroll?"

"He's been in and out of the office since we started having paparazzi trouble."

"What amazes me is the timing. He had only fifteen minutes from the time we put the money in there until all the executives would be in that room reviewing the event," Tyler said. "That's why we put the safe there."

Danita had grown more and more quiet. She was beginning to think about what could have happened if Stuart had not arrived. She folded her arms across her chest and looked at the floor.

Her actions were not lost on Stuart. They were movements he expected to see, but he was amazed at how long it took her to get to that point. He knew it was time to get her out of there and to someplace she could recover.

He walked closer to Danita and eased her closer to the door. He was aware that at that moment what they needed the most was a PR person to deflect questions. However, their PR person and his girlfriend were on the way to jail.

One policeman stayed behind. "I need a statement from you, ma'am."

"Later," Stuart said.

"In the morning?"

"Yes, in the morning."

The policeman nodded and left.

"I'm taking her out of here," Stuart said

softly. He knew she was running on adrenaline and would collapse soon. He also knew that she would not like anyone to see her when it happened. He took her to her hotel.

Stuart was so gentle and understanding, he couldn't have handled things better. He turned on all the lights. He remembered reading that if a person was traumatized, they needed to be able to feel they could see everything. Kissing her gently, he undressed her and nudged her toward the shower.

While the beads of hot water beat down on her skin, he went to the little coffee nook. He read the labels on the tea until he found one that calmed the body so sleep could take over. She needed sleep.

He went back to the shower and held out a huge pink bath sheet for Danita as she stepped out of the shower. He dried her with one towel and wrapped her in another. She was starting to relax. He guided her from the bathroom and she went straight to the bed.

Stuart didn't want to go through her personal belongings and was relieved to see the bathrobe he'd gotten her when she'd become ill in Sag Harbor.

He put her under the cover and lay down beside her. It was minutes before he heard her quietly sobbing. She was now realizing how close she came to death, he thought. Moments later she was asleep.

An hour later, when she awoke, Stuart's eyes were closed, but she knew he wasn't asleep. She shifted until she put her head on his shoulder.

"We have to find a new security plan."

He opened his eyes. "I can't believe it. Your first thought is about work?"

"I can't help it."

"Well, try to get some sleep. I'll be here."

"My mind's too busy."

"Well, while you have security on your mind, add public relations."

"You're right. It's too bad about his employees."

"Can you imagine? You go to work one morning and find your boss is in jail?"

"There's one thing that's more amazing than the robbery attempt."

"What?"

"I can't believe it," Danita said. "You hit him."

"He deserved it," Stuart said.

"I've known you all of my life and I never knew you to be violent. In fact, you were always the one to settle disputes."

"That was with the family. I wasn't such an angel growing up. We Virginians don't talk about those things."

"What made you come upstairs?"

"I went to get the donation money from Wendy. She wasn't there. I remembered you said something about a safe, and that was the only place you could be."

"Did they catch Wendy?"

"She was in the back, waiting for Hugh. As soon as possible, I want you to think about a long vacation."

He was surprised how much they'd been through in just three weeks. Most people didn't have that much excitement in a lifetime. He held her until she fell asleep.

Danita was taking a shower when Stuart left for his hotel to do the same. She applied her business makeup, brushed her short hair into little spikes, and applied mousse. She selected a bright yellow one-button jacket and matching skirt. To finish off the outfit, she added gold earrings.

Stuart returned wearing a business suit, since they had an appointment with Tyler later that day. Before they left, he saw her take a healthy swig of a liquid antacid. He was worried about her tiny body reacting to all this pressure.

"Are you not feeling well again?"

"I'm all right. It's just nerves."

"Do you want to stop and get breakfast before we go to the police station?"

"No, I'm fine."

"You're awfully thin."

"I've always been thin. You used to tease me about it. Let's go."

Her designer clothes didn't hide the fact that she was losing weight. What would it take to convince her that her longtime goal was a foolhardy one? He made a vow that if it continued, he'd drag her kicking and screaming to a doctor or he'd tell Tyler. He didn't like going behind her back, but even if it meant she never spoke to him again, he wanted her safe, and she was one stubborn woman.

She was still a little shaken as they talked to the police. The detective who conducted the investigation was city tough. He asked blunt questions about the events of the previous night. When Danita asked about Wendy, the cop was not sympathetic. He said if they pleaded guilty, Danita probably wouldn't even have to testify. He talked about bleeding-heart judges and jurors and said probation would be a possibility.

Then they joined Tyler for lunch. Since their faces were splashed across the newspapers again, they elected to eat in the company's private dining room.

"We found out that there may not be a trial," Stuart told Tyler. "After they read him his rights, Jackson called a lawyer. The police think they can do a plea-bargain."

"The phones have been ringing off the hook. We played down the danger part and played up the fact that Danita was instrumental in figuring out what was wrong."

"I guess the cousins have been on the phone also."

"You know it."

"I have a good-news-bad-news story."

Stuart and Danita looked at each other. "What happened?"

"The good news is that the board members are very happy. The bad news is you'll be getting a phone call from one of them."

"Which one?"

"You know that a couple of family board members are very old-fashioned."

"Aunt Theresa?" Danita knew how the woman felt about all modern conveniences and that she especially believed that television was the tool of the devil. It didn't matter. She had the right to challenge anyone mentioned as a replacement for Tyler.

"She called me this morning and brought up the morals clause."

"Oh, no."

"She heard about the robbery attempt, but one newscaster mentioned that you two were living together."

"We're in trouble."

The twice-widowed Theresa Lowell Montgomery Benedict had been a force in the company since the late 1950's. She had strong beliefs about the way a young lady should conduct herself, and over the years she had been vocal at all summit meetings. The idea that Danita and Stuart were sharing living quarters without a chaperone was foreign to her. She lobbied against Danita's father and warned everyone that if they did not think of the morality of their children, they failed.

They called her old-fashioned, but they listened to her. Her one vote could not change anything, but she would be heard.

"I'm sure she gave you a fire-and-brimstone speech," Danita said.

"Yes. I believe the word she used was 'fornication.' "

"So, where do we go from here?" Stuart asked.

Tyler grinned. "I have the perfect solution to all of this."

"And that is?"

Stuart waited.

"You two will get married."

Ten

"That's your perfect plan? We get married."

"Tyler, I don't think—"

"Why not? You two seem to be getting along quite well. At least, according to these pictures."

"That's not funny."

"Are you two denying that something wonderful happened, or are you accustomed to one-night stands?"

"Don't bait me, Tyler Godfrey," she warned. "I'm not in the greatest of moods."

Tyler pounded on his desk. "I'm not trying to bait you. I'm just saying that since my little project brought you together, what's the problem?"

"How about love?"

"All love does is cloud your judgment and make you marry the wrong person."

If Stuart thought that was a dig at him, he didn't comment. He did stiffen slightly. Most of the family knew he had made a big mistake with Nikki, and unlike Tyler, the others didn't say anything.

Tyler's veins stood out in his head. "Don't you see, this is perfect. You're perfect. You two make a great couple. You're both workaholics. Do you know how many marriages break up because one partner loves work and the other doesn't?"

"Tyler," Danita said. "Were you trying to do a little matchmaking when you selected us to work on the house?"

The old man grinned. "You always could pick up on things like that. You must be a little psychic."

"It's not going to happen," Stuart said. "You can't just decide that since we work well together, we should be married."

Danita sat on the edge of her seat and stared into Tyler's eyes. "There's one little problem in all your scheming."

"What's that?"

"We both want your job."

"I'm sure we can work something out—"

"No, we can't," she continued. "I don't want a husband more than I want this office."

"She's right, Tyler. There's only one seat open, and the way our great-grandfathers set things up, that seat belongs to whomever is in charge of the New York store."

Tyler's face said it all. He had made a mistake. He'd rolled snake eyes when he tried to get these two together. He'd never counted on their ambition.

"Okay. You're right. But I can change my

mind about retiring and we can all go back to the status quo."

"Or . . ." Stuart said.

"Or you can pretend that you're in love a little longer until I think of a way to get us out of this."

Stuart looked at Danita. "It's up to you."

"I don't mind, but, Tyler, I am not going to help you. If you don't come up with a way to get this straightened out, I will personally sit down with someone from one of those supermarket rags and give them the scoop. For the time being I'm going to commute from Sag Harbor. I feel better there anyway. That should cause speculation that something is wrong."

"Great. Then it's settled. You play lovers, and I'll find a way to break you up."

"We need an office," Stuart said.

"For what?"

"A prenuptial agreement—but in our case a contract."

"Use mine. I need to take a walk."

As soon as Tyler left, they began to laugh.

"You put the fear of God in him, honey."

"He deserved it."

"But we're caught in it. If you think about it, marriage might be our only solution."

"How can you say that?"

"What else can we do?"

"I—I don't know. If we break up now, the

board can invoke that little clause about moral turpitude, and we both lose."

She felt a twinge in the pit of her stomach. The clause was added after her father's scandal. He may have been easily talked into stepping aside, but Danita, on the other hand, was tough.

"Danita, we're good together. Why don't we get married? There isn't anyone in your life whom you want to marry."

"How do you know?"

"Come on, you never dated more than one man at a time. The cousins used to talk about that."

"The cousins talk about everything."

"Are they right?" he asked.

"Yes."

"Tyler's tricked us."

"And we're too avaricous to walk away."

"I spent too many years working for this."

"What if I get New York, Stuart?"

"I don't know."

It didn't matter that they cared for each other. They enjoyed being together, but neither would back off. Danita knew it. She wasn't about to let go just because she was in love. If she got the store, she might find out if Stuart loved her enough to be second best.

"Well, I guess it's time I met your mother."

"You know my mother."

"Not as a suitor for the hand of her daughter."

The pain in her abdomen began, and she

reached into her bag for her antacid tablets. She had only a few left and she was going to need more. She looked up and saw Stuart's face.

"Don't worry, I forgot to take them the night I got sick."

"That's not a good sign."

"It came with the job. I don't usually get stressed," she lied as she ran her hand across her stomach. "Don't tell my mother."

"Let's go to D.C.," Stuart said, changing the subject.

"Let's also tell Tyler he has a reprieve on this."

Tyler Godfrey was visibly relieved when they told him that they agreed to stay engaged and would contemplate marriage for a while. They were going to spend a few days in D.C. with Danita's mother.

A week after their talk with Tyler, they were ready to go. Unfortunately, it was a true Murphy's-Law day. Everything that could go wrong did. They decided to rent a car and drive down to D.C. The car overheated twice, blew a tire once, and the air-conditioning stopped working.

Stuart hoped this was not a preview of things to come. He couldn't believe that he was on his way to the nation's capital to meet a woman he'd known most of his life. She was almost an aunt, and now she was about to become his mother-in-law.

He wondered how their ancestors would feel, knowing that the little store they had in Harlem had spawned a dynasty.

Eleven

The Sag Harbor house had now been put on a back burner. Once the newspapers printed the photos of the kiss, Tyler seemed less and less anxious about the sale. Danita was attached to the house and welcomed the fact that the pressure to possibly purchase it was off. She should have been happy, but she wasn't. She felt as if something had separated her from the real world.

In fact, they had moved the furniture back to its original place but left the boxes in the kitchen nook. That was probably all Tyler really wanted them to do, she thought. He hadn't mentioned selling the house in several days.

Since she'd moved to Sag Harbor, Danita had pulled together a different wardrobe. It was a casual but upscale lifestyle.

She didn't know how to tell Stuart, but she could not stay there and live a fairy-tale existence. Perhaps it was the lie. It preyed on her mind that given the intensity of their lovemaking, there had to be more between them than just being thrown into a twenty-four/seven relationship. They were more than two lonely, needy people who came together for all the wrong reasons. She wanted there to be some right reasons they were so drawn to each other. Was it love? Was it passion that would fade? What were their options if it didn't last?

It had always amazed her how men could make love and not be in love. How they could separate something so important and treat it as something trivial. There was never a circumstance when her body controlled her mind other than when she was with Stuart. Only he had that power to make her forget her dreams and goals and concentrate on pleasing him. Women thought of this as special. Men thought of it as a need they had to satisfy the same way they satisfied hunger. It wasn't so much as what they ate as long as it appeased the need.

Danita decided that it was time for a change. Once they "admitted" there was a romance between them, it gave them a kind of freedom. She spent a day in New York looking at apartments until she found one on the Upper West Side. It was close enough to the store to have an easy commute. She could even walk in good weather. She worried about one thing: the pace. She no longer felt the heartbeat of the city. New York traffic was every man for himself. D.C. traffic was a little kinder to pedestrians and joggers. However, they were both bustling cities and

Danita wasn't sure she wanted to be so competitive.

Living in New York made her step from the comfort of Sag Harbor to the realities of bumper-to-bumper traffic and drivers yelling obscene remarks to pedestrians and the pedestrians returning similar comments, usually joined by a gesture. She had not expected to have longings for a quiet life, and she pushed them from her mind as she tried to think of new ways to startle audiences with future events to prove she was the right choice for the New York store.

If she was startled by her own thoughts of a quiet life, she was astonished at Stuart's reaction when she told him she'd found an apartment.

"What the hell did you do that for?" he yelled. "I thought we would gradually move to the city in a few weeks. I didn't realize you wanted out immediately."

"I just felt that if we do it now, it will take the pressure off us to get engaged. This engagement thing is awful."

"I didn't realize it was a problem. I mean, it isn't just an engagement. We're going to get married in a few months."

Danita shuddered and hoped that Stuart didn't catch the gesture. "Anything that isn't real is a problem."

"What do you mean, isn't real?"

She felt that any explanation would only make things worse. They had decided to get married just because they worked well together. Stuart didn't seem to understand that it was all merely a discussion. He'd never proposed to her. They had simply come to an agreement about doing what was best for the family.

How could she admit that she wanted a real marriage and she wanted it with him? She loved him. She could see herself married to him. Nothing in Stuart's demeanor made her feel that it was anything more than a business deal.

Stuart waited for her to answer his question, but then decided to change the subject.

"Got any more surprises? You're making decisions without giving me a hint."

So that was the problem, she thought. He was afraid of failing, of losing control. Would that make him want New York more? There wasn't a cousin who wouldn't admit that whoever runs the New York store is the king . . . or queen. The only reason the others weren't going for the job is that they'd put down roots and didn't want to move at the present time.

No one said it out loud, but there was also a chance that they couldn't handle the New York store. It was a powder keg, and what happened in New York affected every store in the chain.

They spent a quiet weekend with Elizabeth in D.C. On the way down, Danita told Stuart she'd be working with Tyler more.

"Are you going to be planning more special projects?"

"Not right away but I'm sure if I'm at the store more, I'll get some ideas." Danita's mother could tell by the polite conversation that all was not well. She waited until Stuart was tied up on a long-distance call before confronting her daughter.

"What's the real reason for this engagement?"

"Don't we appear to be madly, deeply, truly in love?"

"Don't be sarcastic. I'm your mother and I know something's wrong."

Danita took a deep breath. Then the words tumbled out. She talked about the mixed feelings she was having about Stuart and her career.

"Are you really going to let Theresa control your life? I think what you really need to think about is what you really want."

"So I'm not going to get any motherly direction?"

"You just got it. I made some decisions I regret but I've accepted that. Are you going to be able to live with yourself?"

After they returned to Sag Harbor, her mother's words kept popping into her head. She knew she'd made the right decision to get an apartment.

She waited until late afternoon before she told him she'd be moving into her apartment, since it was easier to get to work from there.

"Are we back to that again? I thought we'd spend more time together."

"I think it's time," she said. She watched his

body language change. She knew he wouldn't like it but she felt it was best for her. She was going to take her mother's advice and think about what she really wanted.

She and Stuart were in the kitchen, and he began to take out his frustration on the food. She knew he was angry, but his actions were so funny. She bit her tongue and just listened to him as he prepared salad by pulling out every vegetable in the refrigerator. That was his way of dealing with fear.

"I thought we understood each other," Danita began. "I guess what's happening between us doesn't mean anything. I know the engagement's not real, but what about our feelings? I want to get back to my job. You said last night you were to be working with Tyler more, which means you'll need to be in New York more. I know you'll just check into a hotel for the duration, and I don't want to be here alone."

They stared at each other until he burst into laughter. "I hate when you do that. Make me lose control and then just have all the right answers."

"I also have a question."

"And that is?"

"Are we going to invite the town for a salad party?"

Stuart looked at the counter and realized he'd chopped enough vegetables for a small army, maybe even a medium-size one. When he turned back to Danita, his eyes filled with desire, and she knew they were going to have a very late supper, and they did.

Although Stuart didn't like it, they began to spend more time in Danita's Manhattan apartment than in Sag Harbor. He didn't want an apartment, and since they had decided not to live together, he stayed in his hotel. Danita had begun doing little things to surprise him. She'd found out that his favorite candy bar was a Snickers. One morning he reached into his desk drawer at the office and found several bite-size Snickers. He wondered why Danita knew more about him than he knew about her. He'd tried to talk to her about little things, but to no avail. He usually ended up telling her something rather than learning something about her.

He talked to his brother frequently and was amazed that Tyler had done more for Dax in a couple of weeks than he himself had in the years his brother lived with him. Dax seemed to be getting that creative fire again. He wasn't a workaholic and probably never would be, but he did seem to like something more than hanging out on the beach, and for that Stuart would be forever grateful to Tyler.

Danita was spending her time buying the last few items she needed to make the apartment into a real home. She was settling in, becoming a New Yorker. Stuart had helped her unpack and finally admitted he liked the apartment. She had gone to Bloomingdale's and discussed her likes, dislikes and preferences.

They had announced their engagement to keep the press at bay. It was another one of life's quirks to discover that if you're having a clandestine love affair, it's news. People hide in bushes and jump out to take your picture. They pay your staff or household help to give them little tidbits, and most of all you become their number-one priority.

But if you're making a legal commitment, it becomes just another couple story until the wedding. She contacted Vera Wang at her mother's insistence and the gown was prepared.

She'd talked to her mother, who had called Stuart's father, and she began to make arrangements to have the wedding in Virginia.

"I bought one of those notebooks that you have," her mother told her. "I've begun to organize everything, but I promise to let you to look it over before I do one single thing."

Of course, translated, that meant she had made out the guest list, decided on the caterer and car rental company, collected swatches of material, and just needed the date so she could have the invitations printed. Her mother embarrassed her sometimes by being so organized.

She'd tried to mention her father, but she could tell by the strain in her mother's voice that she did not want to discuss the possibility of inviting him to the wedding at that moment.

Danita began receiving calls and notes from

people she'd gone to school with, congratulating her. She laughed out loud when she got a letter from an old classmate, which said, "We haven't seen each other since you came to my wedding." She sent the notes to her mother in case any of the well-wishers were omitted from the guest list and make a note to herself to pull out her yearbook so she could make sure she did not leave anyone off the list who should have been included.

Stuart began to jot down little notes to himself on changes he wanted to make in the business. He began redesigning the Malibu store, gearing the decor toward the young people whose wealth resulted from the craze for hip hop music. While most of these newly rich spent money on frivolities as fast or faster than they made it, there were a few who bought property, restaurants, and clothes, and gave lavish parties. This was where the Malibu store could attract a new clientele.

He'd made a preliminary study and hired a demographer to collect more information. Although he wanted the New York store badly, he was still very interested in the California businesses, especially if Dax would run one or both of them.

Tyler's age had nothing to do with his business acumen. He made the offer to Stuart during a business meeting, in which each store had a representative, about the overall direction he wanted the store to take. Tyler offered New York as a joint venture. He implied that he would let Stuart and Danita take his place.

Skye Godfrey Sylvester had come to New York just to keep her husband company, and since Elizabeth was representing the D.C. store, Skye and Danita had decided to use the free time to catch up on what was happening in each of their lives.

Of all the "cousins," as they referred to themselves, Skye and Danita were the closest. Skye's flamboyance was toned down by Danita's convincing her cousin to look more professional. They had just finished a tour of the apartment and were sipping Long Island iced teas in the living room.

"Umm, I love this drink," Skye announced.

"Well, don't overdo it. You know what happened the last time."

"Back when we—I was single and we used to hang out together."

Danita remembered how they went out for a night on the town with a couple of the female "cousins." Someone mentioned that Long Island iced tea was delicious, and they decided to try it. No one told them how many different liqueurs went into the drink. They flirted with the men at the bar and drank, talked and drank, and continued sipping the drink. When it was time to leave the club, none of them could stand up.

Fortunately, some male classmates of one of the older "cousins" took pity on them. Each of the college men chose an inebriated woman and walked her out of the bar. The girls had wisely come in a limousine, and the men rode home with them to make sure they arrived safely.

That was Danita's last "wild" act. However, this was not the case for Skye. She continued with her wild ways until she met Morgan Sylvester. He toned her down, and her grateful family offered him a dream job.

He'd been with Lowell's GA since their marriage ten years before. He was as uptight as Skye was loose, as quiet as she was outspoken, and as dedicated to the stores as she was indifferent. If they ever changed the family charter, he would be the first person on the board who was not born a Godfrey or a Lowell. She served as a figure head and deferred to all his suggestions. She hated that he couldn't sign the check.

After Danita and Skye spent a little time talking about family business, they got personal. Tyler had warned Danita that if she told one person the engagement was a sham, it would get out. So Danita remained quiet, especially with Skye. The differences between the two women were expressed in what they wore. Each shopped at Lowell's but in a different section. Danita's idea of casual was a black knit pantsuit with a contrasting white collar, while Skye wore an oversized fuchsia turtleneck sweater and white leggings.

"So talk to me about this upcoming marriage,

girlfriend," Skye demanded. "How did you do it?"

"Blame it on Tyler," Danita said. "He asked us to do him a favor and I ran into one of those stringer-type reporters. It never dawned on me he would track me down to Sag Harbor."

"Why did Tyler pick you and Stuart?"

"I guess he picked me because he wanted someone who had lived there. And Stuart is just generally capable."

"I bet your mama's happy. My mama would be wondering why I wasn't married and would bring a stream of eligibles through the house."

"My mother would give me a choice between marriage and going to live with my grandmother."

"I didn't know too much about your mother's people."

"Oh, she's someone who could make you feel responsible for the sun not shining, her forgetting her umbrella, or the fact that women didn't get the right to vote until the Nineteenth Amendment."

"Run that by me again?"

"Even if you have nothing to do with whatever she is upset about, she will look at you and sigh to show that she is so disappointed that you aren't around to make it better. It's that look on her face that says you are not worthy."

"A truly powerful southern woman."

"If she wasn't black, the DAR would have a monument built for her."

"Did your mama make you feel guilty about your daddy?"

"Yes, that was one of the reasons my mother says she accepted Tyler's offer to come live in New York."

Not one to dwell on anything sad, Skye changed the subject "Never mind all that stuff. Talk to me about this man. We are dying to know all about him. When everyone learned I'd be here, they said to get all the information and threatened me if I didn't bring them back news."

"They, who?"

"Oh, Sheila, Gigi, and a couple of others."

"I'm glad I wasn't like you. I didn't have a crush on him. I don't think we could have reached this stage if that had happened."

"Why not?"

"Crushes are for perfect men. You usually get over them once he does something like burping in public. I never thought Stuart was perfect, so I had time to see the real man."

"You want to elaborate on that a little?"

"He's smart, strong, and focused. And for the part that you really wanted to know about"— Danita tiptoed up and whispered—"not in your lifetime."

"That was cruel. You are no fun."

"I know. Let's go out and get something to eat"

"You don't have anything in the kitchen we could heat up?"

"I don't cook."

"I can't believe that you haven't cooked a meal for this man."

Danita hadn't thought about cooking before Skye mentioned it, but she was right. She hadn't cooked for him, and he'd made only salads. Maybe neither of them could cook a real meal.

Skye whooped. "You haven't cooked for him!"

"Whatever. What does he want, passion or pancakes?"

"I hate to be the one to break it to you, but passion is a lot better after you've had a few pancakes. Is there a bookstore around here?"

"A few blocks away."

"Come on. We've got to get you some ammunition."

They returned two hours later with $600 worth of books. Most of them were cookbooks, everything from the most basic book on cooking to books about preparing five-course meals.

"I know it will take you a while to work up to that, but you will," Skye promised. Danita said nothing but knew she'd just purchased gifts for the next ten employees who got married. She wasn't even going to try to work up to five-course meals, but it was easier letting Skye think she would.

They weren't hungry, since they'd stopped at a sidewalk café for a light meal before they ar-

rived at Danita's apartment. They'd each selected a chicken dish, but Danita's was sparse
with lots of vegetables, while Skye's included
spaghetti and was loaded with a heavy marinara
sauce.

"You have to come visit me before the wedding," Skye insisted.

"I don't think I'm going to have time. We
have so many things to do."

"Something tells me there's more."

"I—I've talked to my father a couple of
times."

"What did he say?"

"Nothing much. I did get the feeling that he
wants to see me, and, of course, I want to ask
a lot of questions."

"Are you going to see him?"

"Yes."

"When?"

"I don't know, but I think it will be before I
get married. I'm waiting for him to call me
again to make plans."

"What if you don't like the answers?"

"I'm not supposed to."

"Does Stuart know?"

"He knows I spoke to him."

Skye had let the matter go, headed into a
children's shop to buy something special for
each of her children.

"Morgan's getting nervous about the changes.
New blood on the board could mean a non-fam-
ily member wouldn't stand a chance. He doesn't

really care who gets New York, but he's really concerned about the future of the board," Skye said as they walked back to Danita's apartment.

"Is he difficult—"

"No. He starts these precision antics."

"What do you mean?"

"You'd think he was in the military. Things have to match. The top sheet has to be five inches from the top of the bed. The towels must be a half inch thick. I hope they realize giving him the chance to run the Atlanta store kept us out of bankruptcy."

"But a Godfrey or Lowell has to sign the checks. I'll see if there's anything I can do to make your life easier."

When they returned to Danita's apartment, Stuart and Morgan were waiting for them.

"Where were you?" Morgan's voice was laced with anger.

"We went shopping," Danita explained.

Morgan paid no attention to Danita but glared at his wife. "How could you lose track of time? We came in only for the meeting. Do you realize we have only seventy-three minutes before the flight takes off?"

Danita turned her back to the men and mouthed "seventy-three minutes?" The women collapsed with laughter but quickly got the Sylvesters into a taxi.

"What's with Morgan?" Stuart asked.

"He's always been like that. When he gets really nervous, he breaks everything down to strange numbers."

"I know he wants to be the first member of the board who wasn't born into the family, but he's going to give himself a heart attack."

"He's going to give everyone a heart attack," Danita corrected Stuart.

"Are you staying for a while." She couldn't bring herself to ask if he was spending the night.

"Sorry. Can't. I'm working on a new store idea."

"Tyler wants it now?"

"I'm afraid so."

He kissed her, then held her for a long time, then kissed her again. "Duty calls," he said, and left.

Danita knew that she and Stuart had spent a lifetime challenging, ignoring, and sometimes hating each other, but now, away from all business, they found they had more in common than they'd ever dreamed.

One thing stood in the way of making this perfect. The carrot that Tyler had dangled in front of them—the chance to run Lowell's NY.

She knew she would be disappointed if she didn't get the store. She also knew that she could handle the decision if Tyler chose Stuart. The real question was, could Stuart handle the decision if she was Tyler's choice.

The phone rang. She answered and gasped

slightly as she recognized the voice on the other end.

"Danita, it's your father."

"This is a surprise."

"Your mother gave me your number. I saw the papers."

"Paris newspapers?"

He laughed. "No. Although you are well known in America, you are not that famous here. I still read newspapers from the United States."

"Do you miss not being here?"

"On the occasion of my daughter's engagement, yes. For day-to-day living, not at all."

"Dad, we need to talk."

"I know your mind is bursting with questions. Come visit me, and I'll reveal all the family secrets as well as tell you how to get the New York store."

Twelve

The new apartment was just what Danita needed. It gave her a sense of belonging to the city. She'd even established a favorite table at a neighborhood restaurant.

The living room had great views from a Palladian window and floor-to-ceiling glass doors that opened to the balcony. The room was anchored by a gold-colored carpet. The sofa and chairs in muted shades of brown were placed so anyone sitting in them had a view of the Hudson River. The living room lights were controlled by a dimmer switch to keep a soft look. Every room contained items that reflected Danita's taste and detracted from that "decorator" feeling. She was more and more content each day with the appearance of her apartment.

She was just admiring her completed living room, when the phone rang. She thought it was her mother, whom she had been expecting to call.

"Danita?" It was her father.

"Hi." She couldn't believe he'd called again so soon.

"How are things going?"

"So far very well."

"I—I thought about some of the things we said yesterday."

"And?"

"I think you should come to France right away."

"I'd really like that. When can we meet?"

He paused. "I'll be in Paris for a few days this week. . . ."

"I'll be there."

As soon as she placed the phone in the cradle, she was dancing around the room. For years she had waited to find out why her father had deserted her, and now she would get the answer.

Danita and Stuart were sitting on the living room floor, nibbling the last of a pizza, when Danita told him about her surprise call that day.

"I'm going to Paris tomorrow."

"What?"

"I need closure on a few things." She needed to look into the eyes of the man who'd deserted her.

"You're planning to go to Paris to see a man who has never really been a father? Are you sure?"

"Of course, I'm sure. I'm going by Concorde.

I would have taken a late flight tonight, but I wanted to talk to you before I went."

"Why didn't you talk to me before it was a done deal?"

Hackles rose on her neck. "I don't have to get your approval."

"I—I didn't mean for it to come out that way, but it's just a little sudden."

"For you it's sudden. I've been waiting twenty years."

"I know. I'm sorry, honey. How long are you going to be away?"

"One day. I don't think it will take any longer than that. It's all arranged. I'll hop on the plane, have dinner at his hotel, and fly back."

Stuart could not understand this. Danita and her father spoke once every other year at most, and she hadn't seen him since the divorce became final seventeen years before. "Did you talk to your mother?"

"It has nothing to do with my mother. He left me. Whatever went wrong in that marriage should not have been taken out on me."

He leaned over and kissed the top of her head. "You are one stubborn woman. I told Tyler and my dad that."

"Thank you. But why were you telling them anything?"

"I had to tell Tyler. We're going to meet on a few things in a couple of days, and I mentioned you might go visit your father. Is that a problem?"

"No. Tyler wouldn't deny me this moment even if a business deal were coming through. I just want to set some things straight in my mind."

The stronger Danita felt about Stuart, the more she needed the closure with her father.

"Why don't you just call him up and talk?"

"I have to see his eyes."

"Did it ever occur to you that this might be more trouble than it's worth?"

"You don't understand. Your father did not leave your mother. Your father did not make you the laughingstock of your elementary school."

"Honey, I'm not trying to upset you. I just don't want you to expect a miracle and come back without answers."

She folded her arms across her chest. "I'm not looking for miracles. The only thing I remember about my parents is that they loved each other. I grew up in a house where we laughed, played games, and were a real family. My parents were always kissing. I called it the 'mushy stuff.' And then one day my mother told me my father wasn't coming home because he wanted to live someplace else."

Stuart put his arm around her. He'd never been through that. He did remember most of what happened, but he didn't know the whole story. They quietly walked to the bedroom.

After she fell asleep, Stuart called his father and told him Danita was going to Paris. He was shocked when his father said he was coming to New York.

"There are some important things that you should know, and Tyler and I need to talk to you."

Danita was so nervous, she couldn't sit still when they got to the airport.

"How are you going to keep out of trouble while I'm gone?"

"You will not believe this. Last night when I talked to my dad, he told me he's coming here."

"When did you speak to him?"

"You were asleep. I called him to give him some information, and he said he was coming up to see Tyler."

"Get out of town! Your father 'who-would-not-leave-Virginia-if-the-state-were-burning-down' is coming to visit you?"

"Yep. Now, that's a miracle."

After Danita was seated for the flight, she began to think about her father. Of all the pictures of her father, the one she liked best was her parents' wedding photograph.

Darius Godfrey was what girls now refer to as a "bomb." He was almost too handsome. He had escorted some of the most beautiful women in the world until he met Elizabeth Hemmings, a native of Virginia and the daughter of a diplomat. They were a golden couple and everyone thought the marriage was perfect.

Fair-skinned, six feet, and two hundred pounds, he had a naturally muscular body. But his green-specked hazel eyes were his most startling feature. Darius could make any woman dance to his tune, except Elizabeth. She made him work hard to get her.

They were a fantasy couple, Elizabeth, the southern belle who spoke softly but could be as tough as any man when she was challenged, and Darius, the dreamboat. They looked good together.

Elizabeth had recently graduated from college and Darius was assigned to Lowell's D.C. when they met. They had a whirlwind courtship and a society wedding. Danita came along ten months later. She was a "honeymoon baby."

Elizabeth didn't want to move to New York when Darius was offered that store after his nephew's death, but he thought it was best for all concerned that they relocate. So he went to New York and Elizabeth and Danita stayed in D.C. The commuter marriage worked for a while, but then Darius struck up a friendship with a congressman's wife.

Elizabeth had more time on her hands with Darius in New York and had become involved at the D.C. store. She didn't work there officially, but she would wander through the store and mention that the display in the children's section might be improved or that the clerks

were having trouble operating certain machines
and customers were waiting in line too long.
She never criticized, but made suggestions. Soon
the employees felt comfortable enough to tell
her when a problem arose. Elizabeth became a
welcome sight when she entered through the re-
volving door.

She was a walking advertisement for the
store. Her tiny frame was just right for the petite line. Elizabeth charmed everyone. She realized her marriage was failing, but she never
complained.

Then the scandal hit. Darius and the congressman's wife were caught in a motel. There
was a fire in the motel and everyone had to be
evacuated. One of the photographers took a picture of the guests with blankets wrapped around
them, watching the motel burn. Someone recognized Darius. The picture was enlarged and
the reporter had a dream story. The papers had
a field day. The Lowell's chain became a joke.
People started coming to the store to see if they
could get a glimpse of Darius or Elizabeth. So
the Godfreys and Lowells closed rank and
forced Darius out. He and the woman went to
Paris.

Danita wanted to understand her father's self-
imposed exile. Nothing could stop her.

Seven hours later she was sitting in a little
bistro in front of her father's hotel, where they

had arranged to meet. As soon as he walked in,
she knew him. Not much had changed. Women
still took a second look at him. If anything, the
gray in his hair made him more distinguished.
She saw him flirt with three women as he made
his way to her table.

He took her hand and lifted it to his lips.

"My daughter, all grown up," he said.

She smiled but thought, *My father is still a
child.*

If the paper where she read about the scandal
was correct, he was now fifty-six years old. Her
face, at twenty-six, probably had more lines in
it than his, amazing for a sun worshipper. His
skin was tanned, and he had a loose-gaited walk
that resembled that of a gunslinger. His grin
showed strong white teeth. He was nearly perfect.

It had been almost a year since she'd heard
from him. He moved around so much, she
could never contact him; she just waited until
he called her.

"Where are you living now?" she asked him
after they ordered their meals.

She couldn't help but notice that his clothes
were from the exclusive casual line stocked in
New York, Boston, and D.C. Lowell's stores. The
material was a little too heavy for warmer states.
His brown slacks matched his unstructured
jacket, which fit perfectly. He was one of those
men who looked really good in anything. The

beige shirt pulled the ensemble together. The man was nothing short of stunning.

"I'm living in a suburb now, but I'm representing an artist, and there's a showing here in Paris later this week. Perhaps you'll come. She's very good."

Of course, he would be representing a woman.

"Sorry. I'm here only for the day."

"You came over on the Concorde? I guess the executives are paid a lot more than I was."

"We work pretty hard for that money."

"I knew this day would come," Darius sighed.

"You did?"

"It's like the obligatory showdown in a movie. The moment of truth."

She noticed that he sounded more like a Frenchman who'd learned to speak English than the other way around, but, of course, he'd spent seventeen years in France now. "I guess you're right." She took a deep breath. "Why did you leave us?"

"I was living a lie. I was spending my days doing what my father and Tyler called 'learning the business.' "

"And you hated it."

"Do you like your job?"

"Not . . . always."

"Well, imagine feeling like that every day."

"I might be handling the New York store, but I'm not sure if Tyler will put me in complete control or if I will be in Skye's position—a figurehead."

"Is that what you want?"

"I—yes."

The waiter arrived. They ordered a simple fish stew and a salad and said nothing until the food was on the table.

"You don't really want that store, do you? I noticed your hesitation."

"It would be a bit of a chore for me, but handling special events is what I really love."

"Then why aren't you doing what you love?"

"They aren't separate jobs."

"Make it so."

Time had been good to her father. But there was something he wasn't telling her. How had he survived in a strange land until he learned the language?

"Did you ever regret your decision to leave the States?"

"Of course. I lost you. But I learned who I was and I would never have fit in that corporate structure. It was smothering me. However, before I left, I made sure that you and your mother were taken care of. My . . . behavior in the past will never hurt you. You can have any store in the chain. If you want one, ask Tyler, and I guarantee you'll get it."

"I'll tell that to Tyler."

"If you'd rather have a store other than New York, he'll get you that one. All I have to do is wave my magic wand."

She laughed at the thought of her father doing that.

"I'm going to ask you for a favor," he said.

Danita thought he wanted money and reached for her purse.

"Be very sure you ask for what you really want. Look in the mirror and ask for something your heart tells you would make you complete."

Danita thought about her bouts with stomach problems and how they disappeared once the pressure was off. Sag Harbor had been a refuge. She still intended to talk to Tyler about purchasing Captain's Row. Maybe she wasn't asking for the right thing.

"I read that you were involved with a congressman's wife. What happened to her?" Danita asked finally.

"She lived here for about a year. Then she realized that I didn't love her. She knew I used her to escape from a bad situation, and she was doing the same thing."

"Is there another woman now?"

"I am not a man who can live alone. I was wrong in not informing Elizabeth."

"I see."

"I see something restless in your eyes. You never wanted to see me before. What's happening in your life now?"

"I'm like you. I'm at a crossroads and I'm afraid of making the wrong decision."

"Don't be afraid. Listen to your heart and make bold decisions. What does your mother say?"

"That it is my decision."

"There's something else."

She looked up and smiled. "I guess parents know things."

"I've read the papers, I'm very proud of you."

"It's in three weeks."

"Don't settle."

They spent another hour drinking tea and talking.

"My plane leaves in an hour. I have to go. Maybe we could have another talk one day."

"I would like that."

Danita stood and gave her father a tentative hug. She walked to the restaurant's rear door. Her father had stayed at the table to wait for someone. As a taxi pulled up, she turned and looked back to where her father was sitting. He was not alone. He'd been joined by another man . . . and they were holding hands.

Now she had the real answers.

Having Stuart pick her up at the airport gave Danita a strange feeling of elation. In all her travels, the only one who was ever waiting for her was a limousine driver. Stuart gave her a bear hug and took her carry-on luggage.

"How was it?"

"I got some answers that helped and some that created more questions."

"Are you going back?"

"Not right away. We need some time. He's my

father, but it was weird trying to think of him that way. I've talked to him over the past several years, but face-to-face he seemed more like a stranger."

Stuart and Danita took a taxi home.

It was good to be home. Danita showered and changed into slacks and a pullover and joined Stuart in the living room.

"Did your father tell you anything about the stores?"

"Not really. He said he had hated his job. I guess one day he couldn't take it anymore and revolted. He seems pretty happy now."

"That's good. Did he say anything else?"

"Like what?"

"I don't know. Did he say if he was coming to the States? Was he with . . . anyone?"

"Oh, my God! You knew."

"Knew what?"

"Don't play games. My father is gay. I'm sure that if he hadn't gone into exile, I would be a little uneasy. Since he didn't raise me, I can't get too upset about his lifestyle. What happened when the families found out?"

"The board got together and made him leave the country."

"I thought so. . . ."

She stopped speaking and stared at him. Was this another one of those "open secrets?" Did everyone know but her?

"That's why I'm in line for the New York store. I'm in line for every store in this chain."

"I wouldn't go that far."

"Why not? It must have really been something when you found out I was interested. Is there something in writing that guarantees me any store in the chain? Is that my father's gift to me?"

"What did you want the family to do? They built an empire from the ground up with their bare hands, and your father was going to tear it all down."

"The family? I thought I was part of the family. When were you going to tell me?"

"We weren't."

"Why not?"

"Do you want the whole story?"

"Hell, yes!"

Stuart motioned her to the balcony. He then went to the bar and got a bottle of Jack Daniel's Old No. 7 and two glasses. He poured them both a drink and sat opposite her.

"You wanted to know if it's an open secret. No. Tyler knows, my father knows, and they told me."

"How long ago?"

"Today, while you were in Paris."

"Is that why he came up here? So the three of you could try to figure out something? Does my mother know?"

"Absolutely not. It's the reason she virtually ran the D.C. store until you were old enough to take over. Your father wasn't having a fling with a congressman's wife."

"He was with the congressman! The wife was what they call a 'beard' in Hollywood. So my father was forced to leave and she got money for not opening the closet door."

He reached for her hand and she pulled away. "I've been putting in long hours, working my tail off, just so I could be considered for an opening. Now I know all I had to do was ask. Let me ask again, does my father have this in writing?"

Stuart nodded. "He didn't leave until he had it in writing. There's also a clause that covers your health. They can't make you do anything that would harm you. My father says it's very specific."

"Stuart, tell me the truth. Did you know before today?"

"No."

He held out his hand, and she placed hers in it. The families had made them both victims. If they hadn't had all those hard years of competing against each other, maybe they would have been married by now.

She felt a kind of peace as she put her arms around his waist and rested her head on his chest. Now that she knew the truth, she could open her heart to love. She was no longer in competition with Stuart. No one ever had to know what happened. They'd come together for all the wrong reasons, but they would stay for all the right ones. She didn't feel just passion for this man, she felt safe.

He stepped back and looked at her. The green and gold flecks in her hazel eyes glittered. They held hands as they walked to the bedroom and stretched out on the bed. She slipped out of Stuart's arms for a moment to pull the decorative pillows and spread from the bed.

His lips caressed hers as he gently removed her clothes and then his own. He lay on his back and pulled her on top of him. She wiggled around until she found the perfect position and put her head on his chest.

She was so beautiful. He was so lucky. They were at peace. They could have stayed like that until morning, but as their minds sought and found comfort, their bodies craved a different kind of satisfaction.

Nature took the lead as they rolled over and she was beneath him. Her kisses weren't just seductive, they were life's elixir for him. He couldn't get enough of her moist, parted lips.

"We should stop and—"

"We don't have to stop," he told her. He slid his hand under the pillow and produced the silver packet.

"When did you put that under there?"

"Just before I left to pick you up from the airport."

"Pretty sure of yourself?"

"Pretty sure of us."

Thirteen

She'd stepped out of the shower and found him waiting for her. He kissed her gently. He wore only his boxer shorts, a sexy red that made the undertones of his skin stand out. She marveled as his movements showed off the strong thighs and great abs. She ran her fingers down his torso, enjoying each ripple.

"I missed you so much," he said. His black eyes were filled with desire. He kissed her again. She felt small in his arms, but she didn't feel threatened or overwhelmed by him.

"I missed you too."

He picked up the large yellow, fluffy towel and wrapped it around her. He dried her body, lightly in some places, more vigorous in others. She closed her eyes and allowed herself to be swept away by her feelings. When he was sure she was dry, he tossed the towel in the hamper. He held her hand and led her to the bed.

The time apart had increased their hunger for each other, and they were on the bed, side by side, when her senses returned, but only for a moment. He ran his fingers down her naked thigh and then back up her body to circle her breast with light touches, and she shuddered as the points of passion exploded inside.

He began to drop kisses all over her, causing her whole body to pulse each time his lips found another spot.

Then she used her hands on him, mirroring his movements and eliciting a groan from him. They performed the dance of love as if it were the first time two people ever had.

When he finally allowed himself to climax, she was so sated, she could barely keep her eyes open. "I love you," she whispered before drifting into a deep sleep.

"I love you too," he said as he placed a kiss on the top of her head, and then pulled the sheet over them, and joined her in slumber.

The next morning they were sharing a breakfast of juice and coffee and a variety of doughnuts. Stuart was fully dressed in gray trousers and a wine Brooks Brothers shirt and wine silk tie.

She wore a gold silk kimono tied at the waist. She planned to spend the day doing laundry and cleaning her apartment. She would throw on something else after Stuart left.

"This is not healthy," she told him, looking at her half-eaten doughnut.

"I know. We need to get a housekeeper who will keep us doing the right thing."

"I keep telling Tyler I'm going to steal Jolene."

"He'd hunt you down and take her back."

"I'm sure he would. She's been with him for thirty years."

"Can't remember when she wasn't around."

Danita marveled at the long-term relationship that never went beyond employer and employee but spanned so many milestones in each life— marriage, children, loss.

Stuart looked at his watch and whistled. "I've got to go. I have a breakfast meeting with Tyler."

"Breakfast? What do you call this?" she asked as she waved her hand over the table.

"Morning snack."

"I'll call you later."

"Why does he want to see you? Did he say anything about his successor?"

"We still have some issues with the Malibu boutique, and Tyler's getting ready to head back and help Dax. Now, about the successor, he says he's narrowed it down to two people."

"What everyone already knows. Did any of the families say anything?"

"Morgan's been grumbling again."

"Of course." Danita had heard the same noises from Morgan Sylvester before, so that was nothing new.

She kissed Stuart good-bye and cleaned off

the breakfast table. She laughed as she thought about Jolene. She could never steal her away from Tyler. Danita liked privacy too much to have a live-in. She hoped that Stuart felt the same way. If not, then she would give up a little privacy to have someone else do the tidying.

What was happening to her? Since she'd fallen in love with the one man who had never even crossed her mind for so many years, she changed her priorities. The phone rang.

"Hello."

"It's Skye."

"Oh! Hi, there." Danita was hoping it was Stuart.

"You don't sound too thrilled to hear from me. Did you think it was that hunk?"

"Truthfully, yes."

"No matter. What's going on?"

"Gurrl, I can't believe you and that monster hunk. What's your secret?"

"It's so strange. I mean, I never even liked him."

"I wish I could have seen Nikki's face when she found out. Has she called?"

"Not me. Stuart is still pretty closemouthed about that whole thing."

Danita knew Skye well enough to realize she must have had some hot news and she was stalling.

"I just saw something that might interest you

about the hunk's ex," Skye finally said. "I was surfing channels and came across one of those gossip shows and I saw your picture. . . ."

"My picture!"

"Don't get upset. The announcer was just saying that Stuart was getting married to you and that his ex-wife had just gotten married to some producer or director. You know, one of those behind-the-scenes guys."

"She got married? Stuart's going to love this."

"Well, you did not think Home Girl was going to stay single when her ex found somebody."

"I really had nightmares of walking down the aisle and Nikki running in and dragging Stuart away from the altar."

"Well, I've got to go, but I just wanted to give you that little tidbit."

"Thanks, see you at the wedding."

Count on Skye to brighten an already good day!

Business was no longer the first thing that came to Danita's mind when she awakened each day. Now she thought of Stuart. She thought of spending nights lying in his arms and talking about their future.

She laughed every time she thought about the little things they were discovering about each other. Both had brought some preconceptions to the relationship, and most were wrong.

The first time Stuart stayed at her apartment, he'd been startled to learn that she slept nude; she was surprised that he didn't. After his shower he'd put on the bottoms of his pajamas and when he slipped into bed he'd realized that Danita was totally bare. It had been quite a delightful shock to his system.

Two days later he'd taken her to Tiffany's to select her engagement ring. He noticed she preferred a marquis-cut stone with nothing surrounding it. She didn't like frills. It was one of the things he'd come to love about her.

"What did you think I slept in?"

"Something that covered all of you. Something you couldn't see through."

"Are you saying that you thought I was a prude who covered up even when I was alone?"

"Don't blame me. The others thought so too."

"What others?"

"The cousins. At least all the male ones."

"I didn't have any clothes on when you took me to the hospital."

"Your gown was nowhere in sight. I just assumed that you pulled it off while you were tossing and turning with the pain."

She giggled. "So the cousins stood around, putting people into little categories, like prude, tramp, mother earth."

"Believe me, if they'd known then what I know now, you would have had every Lowell calling you for a date."

"I don't think so."

Now she was back from Paris, with some

ghosts put to rest, and ready to start life as Mrs. Stuart Lowell.

"We still have to do something with the Sag Harbor house," he said.

"I love that house."

It seemed that they were intense people, whether it was pulling off a major business coup or making love. The Godfreys and Lowells never did anything halfway. Stuart was on his way to Tyler's for a breakfast meeting. When he returned, she would break the news to him that she was no longer a candidate for the New York store's leadership. She tried to tell him the night before, but he wasn't interested in anything to do with careers.

Something else bothered her. She remembered telling him that she loved him, but she couldn't remember him saying anything about how he felt. His actions certainly told her that he cared about her, that their marriage would be a good one, but would the loving part be only on her side?

They weren't living together openly. She still preferred staying at the hotel. It was the only thing they'd actually fought about since Sag Harbor.

"People live together, why not us?"

"I don't feel right with it," she'd told him.

"We've had our pictures splashed all over the

daily papers and the rag sheets. What are we trying to hide?"

"Things happened too fast. I need space so I can deal with it. You've been married before."

"What has that got to do with it?"

"I'm an only child. I'm used to being alone."

He'd thought about it and had become understanding about her feelings. He was learning to ask her rather than decide for her. Still, it came back to one thing. Did he love her? She needed him to say the words, but he couldn't seem to. Or maybe he didn't want to make a commitment. Or if he did want to make a commitment, maybe it wasn't to her.

Did he want this to be a real marriage, as she did, or was it just having a convenient woman that appealed to him? One day she was going to get up the courage to ask him.

They spent so many years competing against each other. How would it be now? Could she step back and not push so hard? "Of course" was the answer that rang in her head.

Tyler was a lucky man, she thought. He now had only one candidate for the position he would vacate. She'd carefully constructed her letter of resignation. First she'd give Tyler the letter and then she would make a pitch for special events coordinator for the entire chain.

Danita no longer wanted a job that anchored her to the company every day. Now *she* was the priority, not Lowell's.

She had been part of a family that cared

more about work than anything else. Now she'd
taken a look at herself. There was a world outside the company and she had a chance to discover it.

After a quick shower, she slipped on a pair
of pink slacks and a pink-and-white-striped tank
top and began cleaning up the bedroom. As she
cleared off the night table, she noticed a file
folder that had slipped between the bed and the
table. When she pulled it out and opened it, it
was the demographics part of Stuart's presenta-
tion.

It would take only a few minutes to drop it
off. She grabbed her jacket, purse, and the
folder. As a last thought, she took her letter of
resignation.

Jolene was just coming out the door as Danita
got out of the taxi. The older woman held the
door so Danita didn't have to be buzzed in.

Danita heard voices coming from the balcony,
and rather than call out to them, she walked
toward them. She heard her name, but the rest
of the sentence was muffled.

"Why are you so sure the two of you can't
work something out?"

She stopped and listened. They were talking
about her, she was sure.

"I'm worried about her health." Stuart's voice
faltered.

"What about her health?"

"She's developing an ulcer."

"That's something odd for a Godfrey or a Lowell," Tyler said. "What does it mean?"

"She's killing herself while she chases this dream," Stuart told him. "You've got to stop it."

"I hate to admit it, but you're right. She doesn't know her own limits. When she was interning with me, she tried to do everything yesterday."

Stuart and Tyler had their heads down, but she heard them clearly as they plotted to take her out of the equation. Lowell's NY would belong to Stuart.

It didn't matter that she wasn't interested in the store anymore. It mattered only that Stuart had betrayed her. Well, those two were in for a rude awakening. She brushed her hands down the sides of her pink slacks and stepped onto the balcony.

"I know my limits," she announced.

The two men were jolted. They assumed that the woman in the apartment was Jolene. They weren't ready for Danita.

"He was worried about you," Tyler explained.

"Really? That's not how it sounded to me."

"Honey, you heard only part of the conversation. . . ."

She narrowed her eyes as if to say he had no right to use an endearment with her. The black eyes that had been so full of passion the night before cast shards of anger.

"Just the part where you were betraying a confidence."

"I wasn't. You told me not to tell your mother."

"How smooth. Just the right twist of the word."

"You're pushing yourself too hard," Stuart said. "I'm afraid for you."

"That's not your decision to make." She stepped forward and dropped the letter of resignation on the desk in front of Tyler.

"What's this?"

"My resignation."

"You can't do that," Tyler yelled. "We need you."

Danita put one hand on a hip. "Then why are you two trying to force me out? Oh, one other thing, Tyler Godfrey. You are going to get your attorney to draw up papers and you're going to sell me the house in Sag Harbor for one dollar."

"You *have* lost your mind."

"No. I think I've found it. Now, if you don't want me on the nightly news telling these little tales out of school, make the call."

"Do you want the furnishings thrown in?"

"Why not? They belong to the house. Make it two dollars."

"That's blackmail." Tyler slammed his hand on the table.

"It's not any worse than forcing two vice presidents to work at less than minimum wage.

You think we got into a few rag sheets, wait until they find out about that. They might even get a copy of my resignation letter."

"Wait a minute," Stuart said. "When did you write that?"

"In between kisses."

Both Stuart and Tyler had been caught off guard, and Danita couldn't help squeezing them even more. "Do you know how good I am at my job, Tyler?"

"Of course I do, I trained you."

"No, you don't. Oh, I'm sure somewhere in the back of your manipulative mind you remember how hard I've worked, but at what cost?"

"That's what I was trying to tell—"

"I'll deal with you later," she told Stuart as she turned back to Tyler. "We Godfreys and Lowells have been told since the cradle that we have to be smarter and work harder than anyone else. Most of us have only one identity, who we are in relationship to how we fit into Lowell's."

"You're irrational. I'm not going to accept this resignation. Take a vacation. Calm down."

"You know what the real joke is? I came to that decision in Paris." She turned to Stuart. "I actually thought about my own health. I didn't need you to do it for me." She looked down at her left hand.

"Don't." Stuart's voice fell on deaf ears as Danita slipped the ring off her hand and placed it in front of him.

"I don't want anything to do with this. You . . . cheat!" She held back because the other names that were flashing through her mind were not ones she ever used. She simply glared at the two speechless men and walked out. She knew they had somehow schemed against her and she was pushed out. She was too angry with them to stay and talk. But she couldn't resist one last little jab. "By the way, you are now a completely free man. Nikki got married last night."

"I . . . can't believe she resigned." Tyler murmured after Danita was out the door. "I've got to call D.C. and have Elizabeth talk to her. This is family, she can't just quit."

"I think she did. And what do you think her mother can do? Danita's almost thirty years old."

"All I wanted was for the two of you to see that you belonged together. That's why I paid that stringer—"

"You paid him?"

"Elizabeth and I have been watching the two of you for years. Always snipping at each other. We knew you needed to take a break and—"

"You mean you tried to play cupid and ruined it."

"I guess when you come back from California, you can try to get her back."

"I'm going to take her advice right now. I'm going to put my priorities in order."

"Good."

"I'm going to get her back before I go to California."

"What! I'm going back after the wedding. I know there will be one," Tyler said.

"You and Elizabeth were right about Danita and me. We do belong together. We just didn't realize it. I thought it would be great to be married to someone who understood the work ethic the way I did. It wasn't a marriage, it was a partnership, and if we hadn't gone to Sag Harbor, it might have worked. I just need to finish some personal details there."

"So I guess I'd better call my lawyer."

"Are you going to sell her the house?"

"She didn't appear to be bluffing. It'll be good having her take over the place."

"Tyler, I think you're about to meet the next generation of executive. And if I have my way, Danita will be back on the team."

"Well, that's good, I guess. . . ."

"I've got to call my lawyer to see if Nikki really did get married."

"She was a beautiful woman."

"Only on the outside."

Although Tyler wouldn't announce Stuart's takeover of Lowell's NY for another month, Stuart had to start to prepare his boutique for the transition. Stuart was happy that Dax found the joy that had been missing in his life, was running the store well, and now was pleased to take it over. Or was he? Although Danita was angry, it was the first time anyone had expressed the truth about keeping the chain in the family and the expense that was incurred, not just in money but in personal happiness.

Stuart took the ring out of his inside jacket pocket and looked at it. When they had picked it out, Danita had wanted a smaller diamond, but he had insisted on the flash. She would have to put up with all the press coverage the ring got, he thought at the time, but he would never have insisted on such a large stone had he the chance to buy a ring now.

Living in the hotel was fine, but it was now house-hunting time. If he stayed in Danita's apartment, before the wedding he might delay looking for a house. Stuart was going to love Lowell's NY and why not? This was one of the most exciting stores in the chain. More important, it was the flagship store, the very first one. Together, he and Danita could have been the team to beat every year at the summit meeting. It was a wonderful chance for any of the Godfreys or Lowells. Stuart was trying to give her the part of the store she liked best, Special Events. She didn't know that now, but she soon would.

In three weeks, Stuart had fallen in love. But in his haste to control everything around him, he had gone too far. He'd wanted to protect Danita, and he'd forgotten her strengths. He'd forgotten that the reason he fell in love with her was her strengths, and then he'd treated her as a helpless waif. He couldn't blame her for leaving, but he had to find a way to get her to listen. Surely he could convince her to give him another chance. At least, if all else failed, he could call someone who would help him—her mother.

Once Danita had trusted him, she had shared her innermost secrets. He'd encouraged her to make contact with her father. Maybe it was her size. She was so much smaller than he was, he couldn't help but feel protective.

Stuart knew that what happened had been his fault. He had become a victim of his own ego. He was so sure he was doing the right thing in protecting her that he overstepped all boundaries.

If he'd only talked to her before he went to Tyler's. She would have at least understood that he'd been misleading because he loved her. Now she believed he was a lowlife who used her to get what he wanted.

Tyler had prevented him from running after her. He knew his niece would not be willing to talk to anyone at the time.

The real reason Stuart was so angry was that he knew where he'd gone wrong in the relationship. He'd told her to let him handle things. He'd been so busy trying to rid himself of the feelings that made him vulnerable, he'd pushed all his emotions to the side and made what seemed like rational decisions that would make

Danita happy. Then, when she rebelled, he hadn't known what to do, and so he let her run away, and now he couldn't find her. If there had been a chance that they could have worked together and lived together, it no longer existed. She had every right to be angry and every right to have ended the relationship.

He expected she would have been on television immediately, canceling the wedding. Since she hadn't, maybe he still had a chance.

For Stuart, that meant he had to go back to what some would call the scene of the crime.

Fourteen

Danita elected to stay at the house in Sag Harbor. She bought a car so she could travel when the mood struck. She had relied on rental cars before. There were so many decisions that had to be made. She wasn't sure how she was going to announce the cancellation of the wedding. She hadn't talked to Stuart and she wouldn't do anything until they talked. This should be a joint announcement. Her Scarlett O'Hara mood took over and she put that decision off to another day. Now that she didn't have a job, she had to find other options. She refused to live on her trust fund. Too many of her friends were doing that or trying very hard to find husbands who could keep them in a posh lifestyle. That wasn't her style either. Danita had a lot to offer, and if Lowell's was too stubborn to take her seriously, she would find someone who would show her how to translate her skills into a marketable commodity.

She entertained the thought of working for one of Lowell's competitors. That would really teach them a lesson. She might even take a year off and travel around the world. She probably needed that much time to get over Stuart. This was also a time when a girl needed her mother. She picked up the phone and made a reservation on the Metroliner for the next day.

At Penn Station, Danita walked over to the waiting area and watched the screen that would indicate the track number where she could board her train. It was a longer ride than the shuttle, but it would give her time to put all her proposals together to run by her mother.

The ride was comfortable, and while she worked on her résumé, she was distracted by the scenery and some of the passengers. Cellular phones were ringing all over. The woman opposite her had received three calls and made four.

Danita was relieved to finally arrive at Union Station. It was beautiful, and she was traveling at a low-volume time of day. She took a cab to her mother's apartment. When her mother opened the door, there was a look of surprise on her face. Her usually bandbox-perfect daughter was a slight mess.

"Danita!" Elizabeth said. "What brings you here, and in such disarray? Are you all right?"

"I did something a little stupid."

"And what was that?"

"Quit my job."

"Please, tell me you're kidding."

"Sorry, Mother. Didn't Tyler or Stuart call you?"

"No. They didn't. Why would they call me?"

"The wedding is off."

Elizabeth Godfrey stared at Danita. "Let's talk."

Chris Lowell and her mother had been working on a project, and he appeared suddenly at the doorway, also surprised by Danita's appearance."

"What's the matter?" Chris asked.

Elizabeth didn't wait for Danita to answer him. She took her daughter's arm and escorted her down the hall to a guest bedroom in the impeccable house.

"Do you want a drink? Water, coffee, whiskey?"

"Not right now. It's a good thing I'm not a big drinker," Danita said. She couldn't believe her mother had offered her whiskey.

They sat on the blue and gold quilt that covered the huge sleigh bed as her mother urged her to get everything out of her system. "Talk to me."

They had done this many times before. While most girls complained about how their mothers drove them crazy, Danita considered her mother one of her best friends. She'd feel better once her mother knew they were in for a bad spate of publicity. After waiting all this time for a Godfrey-Lowell wedding, there wasn't going to be one.

"Why isn't there going to be a wedding?" Elizabeth asked immediately.

"I had a fight with Stuart and I threw his ring at him."

"Why were you fighting?"

"Stuart knew that I was having trouble with my stomach. The doctor said I was developing an ulcer. The pressure was getting to me. He told Tyler."

"But you stepped aside. It doesn't matter that he knew it."

"It's the principle of the matter."

"Honey, when people say principle, they mean they don't have a real reason."

"It was his trump card. I was never going to get the store. Stuart knew he could always use that, and Tyler would have to give him the store. He kept talking about trust, but he didn't trust me to tell the truth. He wanted Lowell's more than he wanted me."

"That isn't true. He was protecting you."

"I was ready to give it up. But I didn't want him to just push me out."

Elizabeth shook her head. Her daughter could be so stubborn. "So why hasn't Tyler called me?"

"I—I don't know."

"Because he's not going to make any announcements until you and Stuart sit down to talk."

"So what should I do?"

"Don't throw happiness away because you're angry. I did that."

"But Daddy cheated on you."

"I'm not talking about your father. That was a mistake, but I had you and I wouldn't change that. Three years ago, I met a man who wined and dined me, but I was too afraid to make a commitment. He gave me an ultimatum, and I got angry and stopped seeing him. That was foolish, because I loved him."

"Do you ever see him?"

"No. That's over. But don't do what I did. Stuart can be tough, maybe even ruthless, but he's not a cheat."

"I told him he was a liar and a cheat. As soon as I walked out of the office, I knew it was a mistake, but I couldn't stop. I wanted to strike back, to hurt him, to get even."

"Of course, and you did. But now is the time to put pride in a box and toss it out the window. Call him and apologize."

"He probably won't take the call."

"Last I heard, nothing beats a try but a failure. And for this you should fail several times."

"You're right. Are you going to ever try again?"

"No. But if it happens, I'll be smarter. I'm not going to look for love. You want to call from here?"

Her mother had never mentioned a man who wanted to marry her. She still had her aristocratic beauty; perhaps there would be someone else in her future.

"No. I'll go home."

Danita stayed a few more minutes, then left after assuring Chris she was fine. She went to her D.C. apartment and placed a call to Stuart. His secretary said he was out of town. Maybe it was just as well. He said he was thinking of her health, and all she'd done was accuse him of lying. She needed to take care of some business, her consolation prize.

She called Tyler and apologized for her outburst.

"Don't apologize," Tyler said. "You were absolutely right. We had no business treating you as if you didn't know how to take care of yourself. Have you talked to Stuart?"

"I can't seem to catch up with him. I think he's avoiding me."

"I don't think so. But he's got some catching up to do."

"I want to cancel the wedding, but I'd like to talk to him first."

"I'll have him call you."

"Thanks."

At the end of the week Danita decided to drive to Sag Harbor. She couldn't help thinking about what had happened in just a few weeks. She'd fallen in love, agreed to a marriage of convenience, and then agreed to a real marriage. All that was over now. Her mind kept re-living what she'd done wrong, from running away to giving Tyler her resignation. She pulled up in front of Captain's Row and her world stopped. Stuart Lowell was waiting for her, more handsome than ever in jeans and a sweater.

She knew instantly that everything was going to be fine. Her heart was thumping so loudly, she was sure he could hear it.

"What are you doing here?"

"I came to talk some sense into a very beautiful woman who has caused me quite a bit of trouble."

"You don't have to say anything. . . ."

"Let's go inside."

She walked to the door, but Stuart stepped in front of her. He lowered his head and kissed her on the cheek. Then he took the key from her and opened the door. Once they were inside, he kissed her again, not the chaste kiss he'd bestowed on her outside, but an openmouthed one that she felt all through her body. He then picked her up and carried her upstairs. Instead of going to either of the rooms they stayed in originally, he went to the master bedroom. She almost fainted when she saw that the heavy mahogany bed had been replaced with a sleek, modern fourposter. He didn't let her go as they rolled on the bed and began to make love. In moments, they had gone from being fully clothed to a skin-to-skin contact. They couldn't kiss enough, hug enough. They couldn't even make love enough.

Hours passed, and when they were finally sated, they could talk.

"I know you think I treated you like a child, but, Danita, I was getting scared. I didn't want you to kill yourself trying to be where your father should be."

"I know. I think that you got part of the anger I felt when I knew I wasn't going to be able to run the New York store."

He kissed her hard and then gave her a warning. "You can't keep thinking of me as the enemy. I know that for the last ten or twelve years, that's the way you've seen me. It's a new life now, a life we share."

"So the wedding's still on?"

"Absolutely. And to prove it . . ." He held up the ring she'd thrown at him.

"We are going to be quite a team."

"After I found out what was going on with your father, I did some thinking about how to make my father and Tyler pay for their little deception."

"What did you come up with?"

"We can make them live up to the agreement and give you the New York store."

"No. I meant it when I said I didn't want it."

"We can put a boutique in Sag Harbor, and you could run it."

"Yes." She sat up in bed. "I want the boutique. I can—"

He pulled her on top of him. "Tell me later."

"Good idea."

"I did one more thing for which you and the cousins will love me forever," Stuart could not help but add.

"What's that?"

"I told my father he is never to tear anyone apart again. The little program he likes to put us through is over, or he'll be the one explaining about the New York store."

She nodded and moved closer. "It doesn't seem real."

"What doesn't?"

"The two of us as a couple."

"I don't have a problem with that. Do you realize how strong we are as a team?"

She was about to add something to what he said, but he kissed her, and she was lost in the invisible web of love.

"Is there anything we can do about our stringer?" she asked when she could talk again.

"No. That's his job, to find people in the media and expose them."

She reluctantly accepted this.

Two weeks later they were at the Sag Harbor house again.

"We've got to stop meeting like this," she told him. They intended to plan their wedding, but they spent most of the time locked in each other's arms.

"You're right, but we've worked so much, we

never had a chance to have many clandestine meetings. I think they're fun."

"I think the stringer is finally getting tired of us."

"See, that's the best way to deal with them. Bore them to death. There's just a few things that we didn't . . . uh . . . cover the last time."

"For example?"

"One—how did I know about your ulcer? The first week we were here I accidentally knocked over your tote bag. You had enough antacid in there for a couple of months. Two—did I watch you take them? I couldn't help notice you popping them like candy. I got worried and talked to a doctor buddy of mine. Three—everything I've ever done after the first week here has been to take care of you."

"I know all of those things. I just forgot for a moment."

"Then let me make an indelible mark on your brain. I love you. There's no one else for me."

He leaned forward and brushed her lips with his. Passion rushed through her veins like quicksilver. Heat encompassed her body as if she were caught in a raging forest fire. She couldn't believe that her body could react so. The palms of his hands held her face while he deepened the kiss.

Then he took her hand and led her to the master bedroom. Night was falling, and she could barely make out the bed, but Stuart wouldn't let her turn on the light. He wrapped his arms around her and held her close as he murmured her name over and over.

She didn't remember much about the removal of her clothes. She just knew she was there and he was next to her. She was still in his arms, but his voice seemed far away. Stuart's hands slipped over the buttons on her blouse. The next item of clothing was her bra. He left a trail of nips and kisses down her body, across her breasts, and back again.

His black eyes glittered with desire, and she was amazed at how different this was from the angry glare she'd seen when she hurled accusations at him. Kissing had always been pleasant for her, but she had never experienced the depth a kiss could take her to. She wanted to do something to express her love for him, but she felt too weak.

He unzipped her slacks and kissed every inch he bared. She was his. He didn't know any other way to make her understand. Danita finally got her breathing under control and helped him undress. Her hands slid across one of her favorite parts of his body, those six-pack abs. She could feel the muscles ripple in her hands as their bare bodies joined. She parted her legs and with a moan he slid forward.

"I love you, Danita. I want you."

She couldn't get a coherent sentence past her lips. She was much too aroused. The sensual feeling engulfed her. They made love again and again.

* * *

Stuart shuddered and lay still, then rolled on his back, pulling her on top of him. It took a few minutes for them to catch their breath.

"Set a date. We don't have to do that lavish production. We can get a license and go to city hall. It's your choice."

"That lavish production, as you call it, is waiting for us."

"It's our wedding, what do *you* want?"

"I want us to have a quiet ceremony, but I also want the bells and whistles that our families want."

"So we marry twice."

He changed position again so they lay side by side. "Look at me." Her lids were so heavy, it was a struggle to open her eyes. "This is a forever thing we're talking about. I'll never let you go once you put that ring on your finger."

"That's a mutual feeling," Danita whispered. "I believe in forever."

"Good. Right now I believe in sleep."

He closed his eyes but never let her go. Soon she drifted off with him. She had learned to trust. She had learned that even lifelong goals could be wrong. Now she would have it all.

The room was pitch black when she awoke, and even without moving she could tell she was alone. She turned on the lamp by the bed and pulled herself up until her back was against the headboard. She stretched and yawned. The covers fell to her waist as she stretched again.

"Beautiful."

Her eyes opened. "I thought you—"

"You thought I left?"

"No. I thought you were in the bathroom."

"Been there, done that."

As he came closer, she saw that he held two wineglasses in one hand and a bottle of Tyler's best in the other. He wore a terry robe.

She could see beads of water dancing off his ebony skin. She looked around the room, then back at him.

"I know every inch of you. How can you still be so shy?" he said, and laughed. He put the glasses and the wine down and fumbled around on the bed until he found her robe and tossed it to her.

She took the robe, but instead of putting it on, threw back the covers and strode naked into the bath.

"You're going to get into big trouble doing that," he called.

She looked over her shoulder. "That's the idea." Then she closed the door and turned on the shower.

They stayed in Sag Harbor for two more days. They called the family to prevent them from sending out the National Guard. They talked about children for the first time. They didn't want a large family. They wanted two children, and then they would see if they could handle more. She told him how her father could not admit what he did was wrong. He blamed circumstances, family, everyone but himself. It was sad, but now she could put the past behind her and live her own life.

Sometime during the next week they got their license and slipped into Maryland on Wednesday and married. That was for them. They still planned to have the big ceremony for the family.

The day before they went through the "lavish production," they decided that Stuart and his groomsmen would be staying in the guest house while Danita and the rest of the wedding party would be at the main house.

He waited until everyone went to bed, then sneaked into the main house and knocked on the master bedroom door. Danita opened it and shook her head. He had promised her a traditional wedding, and now he was trying to change the rules.

"You've got to leave!" Danita said.

"Why? We've spent all of our free time together. What makes tonight different?"

"I'm getting married in the morning, and I don't want my groom to see me before I walk down the aisle."

"We've been separated long enough."

"It hasn't been that long."

He was about to protest, when Elizabeth Godfrey appeared and tapped him on the shoulder.

"I think you had better go to the guest house, young man."

"Yes, ma'am."

Danita smothered a giggle as he walked down the hall. She had battled her demons. She was no longer afraid to admit she didn't want the position on the board. She wanted the special events center. Let Stuart make decisions about the store. She would entice people to come in for an event and probably stay to do some shopping. She'd already engaged an up-and-coming rap artist for her next event.

She knew there would be a blacklash because she had stepped aside, but being able to throw away the antacid tablets was well worth it. She couldn't think of that now.

The next morning, she dressed in the Vera Wang wedding gown she'd picked out the first time Stuart had asked her to marry him. She'd almost cancelled the order. She whirled in front of the full-length mirror. Her dream had come true. She had the dress she wanted, the career she wanted, and most of all, the man she wanted.

There was a warm feeling all through her body as everyone assembled at the back of the house. Tyler was giving her away. Her mother had been seated earlier, and four hundred people waited to see this event. Newspapers and magazines had been bidding for the right to attend. She had them all.

She walked into the tent, down the aisle, and came face-to-face with the man who personified temptation.

If you liked
TEMPTATION,
*you'll love Viveca
Carlysle's first
Arabesque romance,*
SWEET LIES.
*The following is
the first chapter.*

One

"If you're not out of my office within the next thirty seconds, I'll have Security handle this." Jesslyn Owens stood up and pulled her body to its full five-foot two inches as she glared at the six-foot plus man sitting across from her.

"Ms. Owens, I don't think you want the police involved," he said. "Your reputation couldn't stand another negative attack."

"That may be true," she bluffed. "But how much negative impact can your career stand? The Senator may not appreciate the publicity this could bring."

Hank Reynolds rose slowly from the chair and started for the door. "This isn't finished, you know."

Jesslyn rested her hands on her hips. "It is for me."

"Maybe you should design a gift basket for people in mourning, something your family might like." He never looked back as he opened the door and left her office.

Her breath caught in her throat at the veiled threat.

A month and a half ago, the first time she'd met Hank Reynolds, he reminded her of an old-fashioned minister, with his soft-spoken ways and his slightly stooped posture. Of course, that all changed when he unleashed a string of epithets over the phone about a missing diskette. Now he'd actually threatened her. She was trying to decide whether or not she should call Security when her sister came in.

"What did he want?" Lena asked.

"What else? The diskette."

"How many times do we have to tell him—we don't have it?"

"I know if I find it I'm going to throw it in his face."

"Aren't we going to find out what's on it?"

"One, that's unethical, and two, I don't *want* to know." She shook off the urge to talk about the threat.

Jesslyn knew that Lena would assume her older sister-protector role if she mentioned the threat, so she changed the subject. Lena, older by eight years and taller by six inches, had always tried to fight Jesslyn's battles, especially when Jesslyn insisted on fighting her own.

"Carolann is not working out as a partner and don't say I told you so."

"You think you have to hook up with her just

because Egyptian Enchantment gave both of you a raw deal?" Lena said. "Hello! She's looking for a free ride to the top. And isn't she the one who brought us the client-from-hell, Hank Reynolds."

"True. But she also brought us three corporate clients," Jesslyn said. "I just meant she needs to spend more time here and less time scouting."

Lena shrugged. "So tell her."

"Right. Well, Carolann and I are having lunch, and I hope we can get around to discussing her pulling her weight or selling her share back to me."

The partnership, less than a year old, had been terrific at the beginning, but now problems kept cropping up, most of them with Lena and Carolann. Jesslyn maintained they were so much alike they were bound to set off sparks sooner or later. Each liked her share of good times with only occasional hard work. Each accused the other of not putting more time in the business, and Jesslyn had to admit Lena was doing a lot more duty in the shop than Carolann.

"What if she doesn't want to sell them or tries to make you pay a lot more to get rid of her?"

"Then I'll just have to find a way to make her so miserable she begs me to buy her out." Jesslyn grabbed her navy peacoat from the closet. "See you later." She hurried through the World Trade Center Mall to the subway.

* * *

Jesslyn decided to buy the suit in the Saks Fifth Avenue window because it had saved her life. For fifteen minutes while waiting for her partner on the corner of Fifth Avenue and 49th Street, she scrutinized the outfit the whole time to keep her mind off the cold. She preferred a conservative look, usually described by her friends as "old-fashioned." This blue raw silk number with a tight skirt, however, would probably leave four inches between its hem and her knees. Although she hated to shop, the suit held her attention and it drew her to the window again and again. The outfit certainly had no place in her Victorian style wardrobe. Yet it was just the thing to startle all her colleagues at the dinner-dance on Saturday.

Jesslyn decided that while her two pair of stockings, stirrup pants and navy peacoat kept her warm enough, she needed to go indoors for a few minutes. It was either Saks or the bookstore.

She opted for the Barnes and Noble bookstore a block away. She stepped off the curb, since the light was about to change for her to cross, then decided to take one more look at the suit. As she stepped back onto the sidewalk, a red Jeep whizzed past her close enough to brush her shoulder bag. The driver took advantage of the slight break in traffic and sped off.

"Are you all right, Miss?"

Jesslyn turned and nodded to the man. The camera in his hand and his pale face alerted her that he was a tourist. New Yorkers were generally unsympathetic toward someone who stepped off a curb on a busy street without paying attention to traffic.

"I'm fine," she told him. "New York drivers hate to miss lights."

The man nodded, unconvinced, and turned to walk in the direction of St. Patrick's Cathedral. Probably going to pray that he makes it back home, Jesslyn mused. Praying wasn't a bad idea for her, either. Not only had she been lucky the Jeep hadn't hit her, but prayer might help with her concerns over her business. Word had gotten to her that everyone was buzzing about her successful comeback one week, and the next that something serious was wrong.

Five years ago, her world at Egyptian Enchantment Cosmetics had caved in. After brooding for a couple of months, she decided to fight back and now owned a small business rather than working as a big business executive. It gave her the one thing she needed: control.

She'd made it back to the top and, while her profits went back into the business, unlike the bonuses she'd once received, the sense of satisfaction was beyond measure. Sometimes, she thought the messenger service, Federal Express and Airborne were really her silent partners. Most of the carriers were on a first name basis with her. That was another thing she liked about the little shop at the World Trade Center—the sense of community among the employees.

It had taken so much out of her when she need partners to handle the expansion. Lena, in her usual big sister bulldozing manner, had insisted on using part of her divorce settlement for 30 percent of the company. Carolann had seemed pleased originally with her 19 percent but lately had been griping about wanting more. Still, business was in the black and orders continued coming in. They'd even snared a few executive accounts. Things were great and still she felt lousy.

The near accident made her decide to be daring. Forget the nagging feelings of pending disaster, she told herself. Buy the suit and go to 44's for lunch. You'll feel better.

She walked through the store, ignoring the offers of perfumed cards touting a designer's newest perfume and the cosmetic makeovers. Her clear, medium brown skin responded best to products of Naomi Sims Salon just a few blocks away. The former model had been the first ebony-skinned woman to grace the covers of *Vogue* years before and she had built a thriving skin care business for people of color. She'd have to call for an appointment and change her look if she didn't chicken out of wearing this suit to the dinner.

Twenty minutes later, she exited the store carrying a white shopping bag with Saks Fifth Avenue printed across it in black and a more than expected deflation in her bank account. "But worth every cent," she said aloud.

Her timing was perfect. She spotted Carolann getting out of a dark green car, putting on her mink and talking to the driver. Jesslyn couldn't see the man behind the wheel, and he drove away just as Jesslyn reached the car. Her partner kept bragging about this mystery man who had made her forget her ex-husband.

Carolann turned, her face paled under her pecan-colored skin and took a backward step as she saw her partner standing there.

"What's wrong?"

"N . . . Nothing." She said. "I didn't expect to see you with a Saks bag in your hand. You hate to shop. What did you buy?"

"That!" She turned and pointed to the suit.

"I don't believe you." Carolann screamed. "All your dresses and skirts come down to your ankles. You planning to spring a new fella on us at the dance?"

"Well, after the suit saved my life, I had to get it."

With that remark, Jesslyn turned and walked toward the corner but it only took her partner a few long strides to catch up.

"I want to hear that story from the beginning," Carolann said. "Let's get something to eat."

"I'll tell you over a burger at 44's."

The two women waited for the light. And Jesslyn had to ask, "Was that your mystery man?"

"I beg your pardon?"

"Come on, you know, the one who makes your voice drop to a whisper when he calls and then you get this really dreamy look on your face."

"That sounds more like your sister's way of describing something."

"You're right. But how about it?"

"I'll tell you right after you tell me about the suit."

Jesslyn checked each corner of the two one-way streets before going across. She would not tempt fate again. They were silent as they walked over to 44th Street then toward Sixth Avenue to the Royalton Hotel. Jesslyn always felt like a dwarf with Carolann. She barely cleared five feet, and her partner was a former runway model. As they passed the Harvard Club, Carolann spoke and pointed to the building. "This reminds me, I asked my ex to come to the dinner."

"That's right. He went to Harvard, didn't he?"

"Yeah. Turned out to be a pretty good businessman before he did the Secret Service bit. I hope to show him I've done okay without him or his advice."

"Did you get his advice when I offered you a part of the business."

"No, and when I told him, he wasn't too thrilled about it. Said I should have let him check it out first. But he gave me the money. After all, it was his idea to tie my money up so

I could have a healthy retirement fund. I don't want money later. I want it right now. That's why I invited him."

"Is he your date?"

"No . . . Uh . . . he's just my guest. I want him to find a way to get my money. But I'm not even counting on him to show up."

"I get it. You want to show him who took his place. Is that smart?"

"What do you mean?"

"You said he was tough and had some sort of nickname . . . something to do with ice . . ."

"Glacier," Carolann supplied. "He's that cold and that hard."

For months, Carolann had said that she was involved with someone, but they couldn't be seen in public yet. Was her ex-husband still pining for her?

"If he shows up, does that mean he wants you back?"

"No way. The man can turn off his feelings at the snap of his fingers. Except guilt. If he feels guilty about anything, he'll try to make it right. It's definitely over. Any woman is welcome to him. He'll show up to check on me. I want him to find a way to untangle my money. He set it up and he'll want to know why I want it."

"Maybe he's changed his mind and wants you back. What are you going to do?"

Carolann stopped and looked at Jesslyn. "He *never* changes his mind, and I don't care."

"Does that mean I'm going to finally meet the mystery man in your life?"

"Uh . . . maybe." She blushed and flashed a dimpled grin. "If he can get away from work."

Jesslyn didn't press the issue any further. Carolann had been saying this guy was everything she wanted and now she was shying away from showing him off.

The restaurant 44's was a big hangout for the fashion publishing crowd, and despite the Fashion Café's lure, it still had a loyal following. They got a table and made themselves comfortable. This was where Carolann and Jesslyn learned the art of ordering a hamburger off-menu from a *Vogue* editor for whom Carolann had done some modeling.

They acknowledged a few people among the crowd of diners, ordered and hardly had time to catch up on the day's projects before the food appeared. The chopped sirloin was served on an English Muffin with little dishes of ketchup, mustard and hollandaise.

As soon as the food arrived, Carolann pounced.

"How did a suit save your life?"

Jesslyn relayed the circumstances without stretching the truth in any way. When she finished, Carolann's stern face gave her pause. "Maybe you should be as upset as that man was."

"Come on. If you live in New York and haven't been brushed by a car you're living on borrowed time." Jesslyn ignored the strained look on Carolann's face and signaled the waiter so they could order drinks. New York was a tough town, but Jesslyn loved the heartbeat of the city.

"Enough about me. Was that the new guy or not?"

"Yes, but I'm still not sure we're ready to go public. It would upset a lot of people, including Palladin Rush."

After she'd left the cosmetic firm, she hadn't run into Carolann until eight months ago, when she'd decided that building baskets was a lonely business and she'd like some partners. A mutual friend, Frank Mason, had hooked them up and it had seemed to be right at the time.

"I'm glad we're partners, even though I'm not a full one," Carolann said.

"I'm not ready to turn over any more of it, yet. In fact, I may have turned over too much."

"We've known each other since you were an executive at Egyptian Enchantment. This gift basket thing turned into a gold mine. I can't believe how fast our accounts are growing."

"That's true. And that's why you, Lena and I need to sit down with a new schedule. You've missed a few turns working in the store."

"I thought we needed more accounts," Carolann's face slipped into a pout. "We can hire someone to run the store."

Jesslyn ignored Carolann's fudging of the truth. Actually, they had a nodding acquaintance at the cosmetic firm and never saw each other socially. It was only when she found she could get a space at the World Financial Center that her friend Frank Mason had suggested she get partners, rather than try to take on the astronomical rents. He'd suggested Carolann.

"We're a long way from hiring a manager."

"Why do you say that?"

"I feel this is the calm before the storm."

Carolann frowned. "Our bottom line looks great. What kind of trouble could we be in?"

"I don't know, but I'd like to leave things status quo until I find out. I've heard rumblings . . . and then there was that call from Hank whatshisname?"

"I told you. I took care of that, and if he has any more questions, he's to see me. He won't bother you again."

"Well, he paid me another visit today. Next time, I'll just call Security."

"No. Don't. I promise I'll take care of it. I don't want to fight with you about selling my share. We can work things out."

Knowing when to back off was something both women understood, and even though Jesslyn wasn't too sure things were as settled as Carolann insisted, it was time to change the subject.

"Is Lena bringing Jeff?" Carolann leaned forward and asked.

"Unfortunately, yes."

Jesslyn's sister had the knack for finding men who were good looking but as lazy as old cats.

Jeff had been around longer than most but he wasn't one of Jesslyn's favorites.

"Shame on you. What have you got against him?"

"I don't know. He's annoying. He thinks he's flirting, but it rubs me the wrong way."

"He just likes to act Big Time."

"He's still a jerk. I guess I just don't want my sister to get hurt again."

They sipped their drinks and were silent for a few minutes.

"Why don't you join the Breakfast Club?" Jesslyn suggested.

"I thought power breakfasts were passé?"

Jesslyn laughed. On one hand, Carolann wanted to be a "major player" in the business world and on the other she didn't want to work too hard for it. Of course, if she mentioned that the women in the group wore designer suits and tried to look business-like and sexy, Carolann would have jumped right in. Clothes and competition made her day. Since Jesslyn's tastes were usually on the nondescript side, they'd never gone head to head in a fashion sense. Now that she planned to wear the sexy suit, she wondered if Carolann would wear something so stunning that other women would pale by comparison.

"But are you going to ignore all that for Lena?"

"Of course. She's always going to go after men who are wrong for her. I tried to talk to her, but she just flips into her 'baby sister go away' attitude."

"You can't stop people from making mistakes. Especially those you love."

"Like your ex? You seem to disagree with his new lifestyle."

"Yeah. Who would want to live on a mountain, for God's sake? Can you imagine the winters?"

"You never said why he quit."

"Remember, a few years ago, some fast food place wouldn't serve these black men?"

"Oh, that! The Secret Service men?"

"Yeah. He flipped. He just walked away. Others stayed and the restaurant got into real trouble, but Palladin just walked."

"Just *one* incident made him quit?"

"Uh . . . he said something about it being the last straw."

"Burnout?"

"I guess . . ."

Jesslyn wondered what would have happened if she walked away from the business world and lived on a mountain. How tough could this man be, if he couldn't handle the pressures of everyday life? She couldn't imagine not being in touch with the things that were happening all over the city. The one thing that she was going to try next would be the Internet. She'd avoided it because she knew that if she went on line someone somewhere would bring up her past and she still couldn't explain how she was innocent and looked so guilty.

"Maybe he's just a guy who loses his cool a little faster than others, or he'd had enough?"

"Are you kidding? *Glacier* is a well-earned nickname. That's why I didn't understand this running away."

"So that's why you broke up?"

"In a way . . ." She looked pensive for a moment then said, "I promise I'll stick with a schedule for the store. If Lena can, I can."

It wasn't the first time Jesslyn had heard that promise. She didn't want to get caught between her sister and her friend. She could only hope that Carolann was telling the truth about wanting to be part of the team. Jesslyn had fought too hard to get back to where she felt good about herself. No one was going to take that away again.

COMING IN APRIL 2001 FROM
ARABESQUE ROMANCES

__HIS 1-800 WIFE
by Shirley Hailstock   1-58314-157-X $5.99US/$7.99CAN
Fed up with her meddling family, Catherine Carson had a plan . . . make a
deal with a nice guy who would agree to marry her for six months, then
divorce. She knew Jarrod Greene was just the man for the job—until he
sparked an unexpected desire. Now, Catherine must discover what she really
wants if she's to find everything she's ever dreamed of.

__DANGEROUS PASSIONS
by Louré Bussey   1-58314-129-4 $5.99US/$7.99CAN
It's been eighteen years since Marita Sommers found herself caught up in a
powerful romance—and entangled in a shocking crime that nearly destroyed
her life. Marita vowed never again to let her heart rule her head. But now,
drawn to a family friend, she once again enters a shadowy world of sweeping
passion . . . and peril.

__A ROYAL VOW
by Tamara Sneed   1-58314-143-X $5.99US/$7.99CAN
As heir to the throne of an island nation, Davis Beriyia's life has been planned
out for him, including who he will marry. Determined to have one last chance
at freedom before his marriage, he disguises himself as a building handyman.
But when he falls for Abbie Barnes, Davis realizes that he would trade his
kingdom for the chance to win her heart.

__DREAM WEDDING
by Alice Greenhowe Wootson
                              1-58314-149-9 $5.99US/$7.99CAN
If sparks aren't flying with her fiancé, Missy Harrison doesn't care—she had
her fill of passion and turmoil in high school with Jimmy Scott. Or so she
thought. On the way to her hometown to finalize the last-minute wedding
details, her car breaks down, and Jimmy shows up in the tow truck . . . looking
better than ever.

Call toll free **1-888-345-BOOK** to order by phone or use this coupon to order
by mail. ALL BOOKS AVAILABLE APRIL 1, 2001.
Name_____
Address_____
City_____ State_____ Zip_____
Please send me the books that I have checked above.
I am enclosing $_____
Plus postage and handling* $_____
Sales tax (in NY, TN, and DC) $_____
Total amount enclosed $_____
*Add $2.50 for the first book and $.50 for each additional book.
Send check or money order (no cash or CODs) to: **Arabesque Romances,
Dept. C.O., 850 Third Avenue 16th Floor, New York, NY 10022**
Prices and numbers subject to change without notice. Valid only in the U.S.
All orders subject to availability. **NO ADVANCE ORDERS.**
Visit our website at **www.arabesquebooks.com.**